ACCLAIM FOR THE QUEEN OF SUSPENSE
MARY HIGGINS CLARK

DADDY'S LITTLE GIRL

"Clark certainly has a few tricks left in her bag."

—*Boston Globe*

"Her best in years . . . a tightly woven, emotionally potent tale of suspense and revenge. . . . With its textured plot, well-sketched secondary characters, strong pacing and appealing heroine, this is Clark at her most winning."

—*Publishers Weekly*

"Few stories of obsession will grab readers quite like this one."

—*Ottowa Citizen*

"A fast and fascinating read."

—*Knoxville News-Sentinel* (TN)

"*Daddy's Little Girl* is the best book Clark has written in two years. Her work seems somehow more solid, the plotting more deft. The . . . ending is so unexpected and harrowing I just had to sit back and allow the story to run through my mind until I absorbed the depth of all I'd just read."

—*Tulsa World* (OK)

ON THE STREET WHERE YOU LIVE

"Is a reincarnated serial killer at work in a New Jersey resort town more than a century after he first drew blood? That's the catchy premise that supports Clark's 24th book. . . . This is a plot-driven novel, with Clark's story mechanics at their peak of complexity, clever and tricky."

—*Publishers Weekly*

"Like all of Clark's novels, this one is a suspenseful page-turner that will delight her many fans."

—*Booklist*

"The cleverly complex plot gallops along at a great clip, the little background details are *au courant,* and the identities of both murderers come as an enjoyable surprise. *On the Street Where You Live* just may be Clark's best in years."

—Amazon.com

BEFORE I SAY GOOD-BYE

"Mary Higgins Clark knows what she's doing. . . . This savvy author always comes up with something unexpected. . . . A hold-your-breath ending."

—*The New York Times Book Review*

"Romantic suspense has no more reliable champion than Mary Higgins Clark. Her characters are . . . breezy and fun, and so is this confection of a book."

—*Publishers Weekly*

MARY HIGGINS CLARK

POCKET BOOKS

New York London Toronto Sydney Singapore

Mount Vernon
Love Story

A NOVEL OF
GEORGE AND MARTHA WASHINGTON

ORIGINALLY PUBLISHED AS *ASPIRE TO THE HEAVENS*

This book is a work of fiction. Names, characters, places and incidents are products of the author's imagination or are used fictitiously. Any resemblance to actual events or locales or persons, living or dead, is entirely coincidental.

POCKET BOOKS, a division of Simon & Schuster, Inc.
1230 Avenue of the Americas, New York, NY 10020

ISBN: 0-7434-4894-4

First Pocket Books printing June 2003

10 9 8 7 6 5 4 3 2 1

POCKET and colophon are registered trademarks of
Simon & Schuster, Inc.

For information regarding special discounts for bulk purchases,
please contact Simon & Schuster Special Sales at 1-800-456-6798
or business@simonandschuster.com

Frontispiece image © 2002 Corbis
All other images used courtesy of the Mount Vernon Ladies' Association
Front cover illustration by Tom Hallman

Printed in the U.S.A.

In joyful memory of Warren
and for Marilyn, Warren, David, Carol and Patty
who are the best of both of us

Dear Reader:

I grew up with the idea that George Washington, our first president, was both pedantic and humorless. That notion was fostered by the quotes attributed to him, such as, "Father, I cannot tell a lie; I chopped down the cherry tree."

When, as a radio scriptwriter, I researched the life for a historical series I was writing, I was surprised and delighted to find the engaging man behind the pious legend. The self-righteous quotes attributed to him were all fabrications of Parson Weems, an after-dinner speaker who made his living inventing stories about Washington after Washington's death. The pity is, the truth would have served him better.

Washington was a giant of a man in every way, starting with his physical height. In an era when men averaged five foot seven inches, he towered over everyone at six foot three. In my research, I learned that our first president was the best dancer in the colony of Virginia. He was also a master horseman, which was why the Indians gave him their highest compliment: "He rides his horse like an Indian."

I had always believed that he married an older woman, a widow, and that his true love was Sally Carey, his best friend's wife. The fact is that George and Martha loved each other deeply. Yes, she was older, but only three months older than he, twenty-seven to his twenty-six when they were married. For the next forty-two years she shared his life in every way. She crossed the British lines to join him in Boston, and she endured with him the bitter hardship of the winter in Valley Forge. As Lady Bird Johnson was never called Claudia, Martha Washington was never known as Martha. Her family and friends called her Patsy. George always called her "my dearest Patsy" and wore a locket with her picture around his neck.

Mount Vernon Love Story is my first book, a biographical novel about two people I came to respect and love. It was published in 1969 under the title *Aspire to the Heavens,* which was the family motto of Washington's mother. All the events, dates, scenes and people are based on verified historical research.

I am delighted that this novel is being reissued now.

I do hope you enjoy reading it as much as I enjoyed writing it.

Sincerely,

Mary Higgins Clark

Mount Vernon
Love Story

IT WAS A WINDSWEPT, RAW MARCH MORNING and the city looked bleak and dreary as it shivered under the overcast sky. But the man who stood at the window of his study in the large house on Market Street didn't hear the rattling of the wind against the panes or even feel the persistent draft that penetrated between the window frame and sill. He was staring unseeingly into the street.

In his mind he was hundreds of miles away and just arriving at Mount Vernon. Eagerly he pictured the last few minutes of that journey. The carriage would gather speed as the horses galloped up the winding road. Then they'd round the bend and it would be there . . . the great house, gleaming and white in the afternoon sun.

For years he'd looked forward to that homecoming. Several times during severe illness he'd thought that he wouldn't live to enjoy Mount Vernon. But now the hour was at hand. Now he could go home.

He was a tall man who still carried himself impressively well. When he was twenty-six an Indian chief had exclaimed that he walked straighter than any brave in the tribe. At sixty-five he'd begun to bend forward a little like a giant tree that could no longer resist the battering force of the wind.

The width of his shoulders was still there, although the shoulders no longer suggested the agile strength that had once made him seem near godlike to an army. The long white hair was caught in a silk net at the nape of his neck. The black velvet suit and pearl-colored vest had become almost a uniform. The days of blues and scarlets were behind him.

He was so absorbed in his thoughts that he didn't hear the light tap on the study door, nor did he note when the door opened. For a long moment Patsy stood surveying him intently. To her worried eyes he seemed weary and gaunt. But beneath the concern a current of joy rippled and danced through her. Her fears had been groundless! For eight years a persistent instinct had nagged her that something would happen to him . . . that he wouldn't live to go home with her . . . but she'd been wrong. Thank the dear, dear God, she'd been wrong.

She was a short woman. The gently rounded figure that had once made her seem doll-like had thickened into solid matronly lines. Still, she moved with a quick, light step and from under her morning cap silvery ringlets lined her forehead giving her a disarmingly youthful look. Long ago she'd explained to the man she was watching that even though her name was Martha, her father had dubbed her Patsy because he thought Martha too serious and weighty. Now this man was almost the only one left who called her Patsy.

She started across the room and went up to him. "Are you ready to go?" she asked. "It's getting late."

He turned quickly, looked puzzled for an instant, then wrenched himself back into the present. With a sheepish expression he reached for his black military hat and yellow kid gloves. "Indeed, after professing to have longed for this day, it would seem unfit to be tardy for my deliverance," he commented wryly. He pulled on his gloves then sighed, "It really is over, isn't it, Patsy?"

For a moment her expression became anxious. "You don't mind giving up, do you, my dear? You're surely not sorry that you didn't accept another term."

He put his hat under his arm and now his eyes twinkled. "My dear, if John Adams is as happy to enter this office as I am to leave it, he must be the happiest man in the world."

Lightly he touched his lips to her cheek. "I won't be long," he told her, "and then if Lady Washington will not mind spending her afternoon with a private citizen . . ."

"I wish I were going with you now," she said.

He shook his head. "Since Mrs. Adams couldn't be here to watch John take the oath of office, your presence might point up her absence."

Then he was gone. His valet, Christopher, was waiting downstairs to open the front door. Usually Christopher said, "Good-bye, Mr. President," but now he only bowed. The words had trembled and died on his lips as he realized that he would never be saying them again. But after he closed the door behind the tall old gentleman, he whispered softly, "Good-bye, Mr. President."

The wind whipped around the wide-rimmed black hat. He raised his hand to steady it, then quickly braced himself and with a rapid stride started down the block. A small cluster of people were waiting on the street just beyond the grounds of the executive mansion. They bowed and he nodded to them. He heard their footsteps behind him as he turned in the direction of Federal Hall.

The full blast of the March gale pushed hard against him and he leaned forward slightly. He had a fleeting thought that he should have ordered the carriage, but it was a relatively short walk and there was something about going to this ceremony on foot that appealed to him. It was less obtrusive and he wanted to be unobtrusive now.

Maybe he needed this bit of solitude, too. One had to adjust to the end of the road as thoroughly as one adjusted to its beginning.

The beginning . . . In a way it seemed only yesterday that his mother had warned him about always dreaming and never accomplishing. But it wasn't yesterday. That was over fifty years ago when he was a lad of twelve or thirteen and back at Ferry Farm.

The coldness of the March air faded into the bleak chill of a forbidding parlor. The crunching of his boots became the tapping of his foot on the uncarpeted floor-boards. The stark branches of the trees took on the appearance of the depressing furniture in his mother's home. He was absorbed in the memory of that home as he continued on the last walk he would ever take as President of the United States . . .

HIS FOOT TAPPED AGAINST THE FLOOR AS he sprawled uncomfortably on one of the stiff old chairs in the parlor at Ferry Farm. As always he'd had a time becoming absorbed in his book. There was something forbidding and uncomfortable about the spartanly furnished room, about the house itself.

He was a scant thirteen but had already decided that when he grew up, his home would be warm and welcoming. It would have fine papers on the walls and a marble chimney, papier-mâché on the ceilings and neat mahogany tables which could be joined together for company. George spent much time envisioning that home.

Sighing, he turned back to his reader. Once more he shifted, trying to find a comfortable position. There simply didn't seem to be room enough for his legs anymore—in the past year he'd gained three inches, was now nearly 6 feet 1 inch, and did not seem to be finished growing. Even his shoulders were pushing their way out of the plain shirting that his mother considered suitable garb.

His book that day was the *Young Man's Companion*. His favorite lines in it were:

> *Get what you get honestly.*
> *Use what you get frugally.*
> *That's the way to live comfortably*
> *And die honorably.*

The book slid from his lap. He would have a useful life. Long ago he'd promised his mother that he'd live up to her family's motto. Mary Ball Washington was a difficult woman to please, but that promise had pleased her and evoked one of her rare moments of tenderness.

George thought again of the story he'd heard of when his mother first came into this house as a bride. His father carried her over the threshold and the first thing her eye fell on was the family copy of Matthew Hale's *Contemplations*. The housekeeper had left the book open at the page that bore the signature of her husband's first wife.

Mary Washington said to her husband, "Put me down, please." Firmly she walked over to the book, picked up a pen, and wrote her own name, boldly and with flourishes. The new mistress was very much in charge from that day on.

George loved his mother but he didn't like her very much. Since his father's death when George was eleven he'd tried to be the man of the house for her, but Mary Washington allowed no smidgen of authority to be taken from her even by her own son. She took care of her brood, wrangled with the overseers who handled the vast lands her husband had left to her and the children, and carried a leather whip at her belt to ensure obedience from her offspring.

George had an uneasy conscience about the fact that he was much happier during his long visits to his half brothers Augustine and Lawrence. They lived on their own estates now. Lawrence on the Hunting Creek land that he'd renamed Mount Vernon, and Augustine on the Rappahannock Farm near Fredericksburg.

Both young men seemed to understand George's feelings because he was frequently invited to spend long periods of time with them. "And how is your good mother?" Lawrence would ask when George arrived. "The same?"

"The same," George would say, hoping that a wry note did not creep into his voice. He wished he could love his mother more. And then he'd forget her and settle into the comfortable atmosphere of his brothers' homes and families.

Now his mother stalked into the room. "Idle?" Her spare figure was even straighter than usual. The nostrils of her roman nose suggested a sniff . . . always a dangerous sign.

George sprang up. "No, madame. I have been reading my meditations." Lamely he pointed to the book which had slid unnoticed to the floor.

His mother picked it up. "It is not enough to read about how to live life, or to dream it. It is quite more important to do something about it. Are your chores finished?"

"Yes, Mother." He hesitated a moment. It was probably a dangerous time to bring up a sore subject but intense desire to know his mother's mind pushed him on. "And, Mother, have you given further thought to my going to sea?"

It was the wrong time. His mother's eyebrows, thick and well-shaped, drew into an almost unbroken line. "I see no need to think about it today. I have at least three years longer to give that subject my thoughts." She turned and stalked from the room.

She'd only been gone a moment when his sister Betty slipped in. "Is she vexed with you again?" Betty asked anxiously.

George smiled a welcome. Betty was only a year younger than he and they'd always been close. He wondered again how she had ever been their mother's daughter. Betty was pretty, gay, and lighthearted. She always had a light novel tucked in her workbasket. She never walked but seemed to dance across a room. Oddly, of all the children, she got along best with the mother.

She and George understood each other completely and shared dreams. Betty, too, had her own ideas about her future home. "I shall have the very grandest house in all Fredericksburg," she often said. "It shall be built just for me and have great beams and fine brass, a beautiful reception hall with lovely, lovely furnishings. And I shall be the mistress in the finest gowns from London. I'll have lots of company and be very gay all the time and not live like this." Whenever she got to that part of her dream, she would give a near sniff and look greatly like her mother.

Now she stood in front of her tall brother and looked at him adoringly.

George cupped her chin in his hand. "God help the young men in a year or two. No, little one, she isn't really vexed. She just wants to get vexed about something, so beware."

Betty giggled. "Well, if she goes to the kitchen, she'll have plenty of reason. Cook's new assistant has vastly overcooked the pork and cook is in a state."

George groaned. "Dinner should be a pleasant affair indeed. Thank God I'm off for Mount Vernon tomorrow."

Betty sighed. "I'm glad for you but how I shall miss you. You love Mount Vernon very much, don't you?"

George considered a moment. "Yes," he said. "Lawrence and Anne are so kind to me but it's more than that. That land . . . just the way the sun shines on it, or the snow blankets it in white. The way it looks in autumn when the great trees are losing their leaves. It's the joy of riding across the acres next door to Belvoir and visiting with the Fairfaxes. It's riding home again late, when evening shadows are touching the house and the sun is sinking and the Potomac is half dark, half gleaming. Yes, Betty, I truly love Mount Vernon."

T HE FIRING OF THE CANNONS BROUGHT him sharply back to the present. Of course, the cannons were being fired to signify the momentous event that was about to take place. For a moment he thought of the cannons that had purchased this moment—the ones that had shattered the silence of '74 and '75.

There was a great crowd outside the building of the Congress. It parted quickly to let him pass. He began to climb the steps. And then the applause began. It started tentatively, one single pair of hands clapping, then like a flash it swept through the assemblage.

The sound preceded him so that when he came in sight of the lower chamber of the House, the members were already on their feet. A burst of applause greeted his entrance. It rose in volume and pushed against the ceiling and walls of the great room. It mingled with the ovation which the people outside continued to offer.

He quickened his pace, anxious to reach his seat so that the tribute might end. "Not for me," he thought. Not today. But when he reached his place and stood there the tremendous sound didn't abate; it reached a crescendo then softened and died reluctantly.

Jefferson was the next to arrive. The President watched as the tall aristocratic figure made his way through the room. He was wearing a long blue frock coat and his even patrician features betrayed none of the turmoil that might well be expected of the Vice-president-elect.

They had often opposed each other in their views, so much so that Jefferson had resigned from the cabinet. But George eyed his old friend affectionately. He would not admit, even to himself, that much as he and Jefferson had differed in many ways, he could warm to the man far better than he could to John Adams.

He thought of the day in '76 when the messenger had come to his New York headquarters, bearing a copy of the Declaration of Independence. He'd opened it slowly. For months he'd been begging for a statement like this and fearing it would never come. Even after a year of conflict some members of Congress still talked about an eventual reunion with England. He'd tried to point out that armies must fight for a cause; they must have a goal. Independence was a mighty word. It made it possible for a man to put up with starvation and misery. It drove out fear. And still many of the lawmakers vacillated about making a final break with the mother country.

Finally he'd been promised that a formal document would be issued. In the hopelessness of that first New York campaign he waited for it and wondered just how weak and carefully hedged it would be. The news that Tom Jefferson was charged with the responsibility of writing it made him cautiously optimistic. Jefferson was young but he wrote with the bold pen of a dedicated man. Then when he read the Declaration and absorbed the full richness and power of it, the majesty and breathtaking vision of it, he exultantly ordered that it be proclaimed to all the troops. That evening he stood at the door of headquarters and watched the expressions on the men's faces as a booming voice cried: "When in the course of human events . . ."

A stirring in the chamber announced the fact that the President-elect had arrived. George knew that Adams had ordered a new coach-and-four for this day. He'd refused to let even Patsy make him comment on the fact, but had been content to remind her that they had had a new carriage at the beginning of the first term in New York.

Patsy had sniffed that there was something about Adams that made you fairly feel as though he should be riding in front with the groom. Again George declined to answer. In the secret recess of his soul he quite agreed.

John was a powerful patriot with a brilliant mind, but there was something about the man's attitude toward himself, at once obsequious and resentful, that was curiously irritating.

Adams was wearing a handsome pearl-colored broadcloth suit. His sword gleamed at his waist. But his expression was as dour as ever. A pity Mrs. Adams could not be here, George thought. Only she seems to have the talent for putting John at ease.

Eight years before, Adams had been embarrassed when greeting George, who was to take the oath of the Presidency. Now once again he seemed embarrassed. His nod was nearer to a bow. He seemed too hasty to begin his Inaugural Address.

George settled back slightly in his chair. It was understandable, the man was nervous. He thought of his own first Inauguration. He remembered the crimson velvet cushion that had held the large leather-covered Bible . . . the cheers of the crowd . . . his own opening words: "No event could have filled me with greater anxiety than that of which the notification was transmitted by your order . . ." He'd wanted them to know that he entered the office aware that he might fail them. Had he failed them? He hoped not.

Years ago he'd sworn that he would do well.

Years ago.

Just suppose it had all worked out that he had been able to go to sea. How different his life might have been. Nearly fifty years ago he'd wanted a nautical career so desperately but his mother refused him her permission. He sighed deeply. Even now, like a learned response, the pulsing anger of that moment came back—the fury, the frustration, the sense of dead end. He leaned forward a bit but he wasn't hearing John Adams' address. The rather flat nasal voice seemed to become more clipped and sharp-toned . . . It became his mother's voice.

IT WAS TO LAWRENCE DURING A VISIT TO Mount Vernon that he'd first confided his ambition to become a seaman. Lawrence had agreed with the idea completely, deeming a career at sea "a useful experience."

For George the approval of his half-brother, whom he admired very much, had been the final factor in his decision. Lawrence was everything George ever hoped to be himself—a courtly host, well-read, excellent on horseback, an adventurer, a member of the House of Burgesses. Lawrence had had a brief but distinguished military career as Captain of the Marines on the flagship of Lord Vernon during the siege of Cartagena in '42. And with Lawrence's help he might be able to get his mother's permission.

Lawrence consented to write a note which George brought back to Ferry Farm. The persuasive note had seemed to do the trick. Begrudgingly his mother gave the long-awaited consent. She even had his father's old chest hauled into his room and attended to his packing. She did not tell him that in her last letter to her brother,

Joseph Ball, in England, she'd sought his advice on the subject.

Joseph Ball's answer was exactly in keeping with his irascible nature. He suggested that she might just as well apprentice her son to a tinker.

When the letter came, it hardened Mary Washington's wavering uncertainty into solid decision. She came to George's room, ordered him to unpack, and said there would never be further discussion on the subject.

George stared at his parent, thunderstruck. He could not believe what he'd heard. Then, realizing that there was not the faintest chance of changing his mother's mind, he stormed out of the house, not caring that the door banged wildly behind him.

With lightning speed he saddled his horse. A sharp smack against the animal's side sent it galloping across the field. Harder . . . Faster . . . The wind stung his face. How dare she? How dare she? The hoofbeats were in cadence with his angry thoughts. Keeping him waiting, half promising, changing her mind . . . finally promising. Then at the very moment he was about to go doing a complete about-face on the word of an uncle he hadn't laid eyes on in years.

The injustice! The unfairness! Faster . . . Faster . . . Faster . . . The horse came to a stone wall and unhesitantly scaled it. Distracted for the moment, George bent down and patted the animal's neck. "Good girl," he murmured, then realizing that the horse was sweating profusely, he pulled in the reins and slid to the ground.

He was on the high country and could look down on the farmhouse. The peacefulness of the scene made the fury slowly dissipate and a sense of melancholy took its place. He realized that being at this spot was not an accident. Subconsciously he'd been heading here all the time.

The year before his father died they'd ridden here together. That was six years ago, when he was ten, and still smarting from the sting of his mother's switch across his legs. His father said nothing till they dismounted, then told him, "Your mother is quite right that your temper must be controlled. She seems to feel it can be accomplished by making you afraid to give in to it. I feel that you must govern it for a different reason—because you are growing up and it is unmanly and unseemly for you to have temper outbursts."

At that point his father came directly up to him and put both hands on his shoulders. "You have strong feelings, my son. Channel them to good," he said. "You have passionate anger. Channel that into accomplishing manly deeds."

In a way the words had bitten more than the rawhide whip. His display of temper had evoked an even stronger display from his mother. Therefore, he'd reasoned, why should he be punished? But his father's words, spoken as they were, with understanding and sadness made him say, "I will try . . . I will honestly try."

From that day till this one he'd carefully curbed his easily aroused anger. And now how could he channel this feeling into accomplishing a manly deed? He wanted to see the world. He wanted to achieve. He didn't want to stay here, neither boy nor man, held down, checked, the object of his mother's whims.

Despairingly his eyes swept the countryside. This farm would become his when he was twenty-one. Already he'd gotten his father's rusty surveyor's tools out of the old shed and had begun to practice with them. Already he'd marked off the boundaries of his own land and had even helped his cousins with theirs.

And beyond this little cluster of farms lay millions of uncharted acres—virgin territory with rich soil and fine lumber. Surveyors were already beginning to explore it, choosing for themselves the most select property. In a generation they'd be men of wealth and substance.

The thought repeated itself. Could that be the answer? Could not this magnificent country offer even more chance for high adventure and advancement than a life at sea? Surveying was an honorable profession and a valuable one to a landowner. Slowly George mounted his horse and through the gathering dusk rode home.

The family ate in the large entrance room that doubled

as a dining room. His mother looked up from the head of the table when he opened the door and rose abruptly. "In here." With a jerk of her capped head, she indicated the sitting room to the left.

Dutifully he followed her in. Since she did not sit down, he too ignored the stiff leather chairs and remained standing. From his great height she seemed small and for the first time, her steely eyes and tight-lipped expression did not intimidate him. "Madame," he said, "I humbly beg your pardon."

There was no relenting in her manner. "It is well that you realize that you have much to beg pardon for. You are not so old, nor so big, that I couldn't make you dance to a pretty tune." Her left hand significantly tapped the whip at her belt. "And do you think I would tolerate any child of mine, of any age, flaring from my presence with doors banging and feet clattering on the stairs?"

Even the tart, unbending retort could not irritate him now. He was suddenly very sorry for this straight-backed woman and mindful of how difficult life must be for her. Ever since his father's death, mismanagement had been dissipating much of the value of the great acres of land that was the family inheritance. His mother was simply incapable of commanding the loyalty and devotion of her overseers and slaves. In her constant fanaticism about minute details she utterly overlooked the overall failure of the manner in which her affairs were handled. It was time, he reflected, that as her oldest son he tried to help her instead of constantly judging her.

"Mother," he said quietly, "I will never again mention any desire to go to sea. Instead I will direct my efforts to surveying and seek to obtain a surveyor's license. The more I know about land, the better I shall be able to eventually handle our own property and add to it."

If he had expected approval, he was disappointed. "High time you started considering a sensible occupation," his mother snapped. "Provided, of course, this is not yet another of your enthusiasms. Now come out to your dinner."

He held her chair at the table, then took his own place and answered Betty's anxious glance with a wink. No, it is not an enthusiasm, he told himself. It is a future. He could hardly wait for his next visit to Mount Vernon. Lawrence would want to know . . .

Lawrence not only applauded the plan, but immediately took concrete steps to further it. Pointing his hand in the direction of Belvoir, he said thoughtfully, "Colonel Fairfax is sending trained surveyors to the Shenandoah Valley on an expedition for Lord Fairfax. It would be excellent experience for you if you were included in the party."

George felt his face flush with excitement at the prospect. Unseemly bursts of emotion, he warned himself.

He was proud that when he spoke, his voice was level and controlled. "Do you think there might be a possibility?"

"Let's ride over to Belvoir and see the colonel," Lawrence proposed. "He already likes you very much and, after all, he is my father-in-law."

Colonel Fairfax was in his study. With a nod to his secretary he dismissed the man and his entire attitude suggested that he'd been hopeful of this visit all day. "Well, well," he said, "it's good to see my young friend back with us again. And Lawrence—I trust you're still being a good husband to my daughter. I haven't seen her in three days, you know."

Lawrence laughed. "Anne is an angel, as usual, sir. And in good spirits, too."

The colonel looked serious. "Let us pray the Almighty will allow the baby she is carrying to live and thrive. It's a crushing heartbreak for a young mother to lose three infants." He changed the subject abruptly. "Now, young Washington, I'm told your seafaring career has been nipped in the bud. What's the next step? And for heaven's sake, sit down. I'm not His Majesty, you know."

George laughed and selected a chair that would give him room to stretch his long legs. He had a fleeting hope that he'd finally stopped growing. Six feet three and a half was quite enough body to try to manage. As usual he felt his shyness melt in the presence of the affable colonel.

"I've decided to be a surveyor, sir," he explained. "I've been using my father's tools this past year and I believe I can do accurate work."

Colonel Fairfax slapped his hand on his desk. "Excellent. As a matter of fact I'm sending George William on an expedition to mark my cousin's acreage down the south bend of the Potomac and into the Shenandoah. They'll be gone about a month. Perhaps you'd consider accompanying the party."

"That's why I'm here, sir," George said simply.

"Then it's settled. It will be good experience for you and you'll be good company for my son. Do you agree, Lawrence?"

Lawrence nodded. "My brother is chafing to become a man. I think he'll get his initiation with the kind of camping out they'll be doing."

George was pondering the idea of being a companion to George William Fairfax. Secretly he was in total awe of the handsome, suave young man who was seven years his senior. Someday he too would dress with the easy grace of George William; he too would always say the right thing at the right moment; he too would inspire respect and devotion from his underlings.

"Yes, it will be good for both of you," Colonel Fairfax mused. "My son is paying court to Wilson Carey's daughter, Sally, from over near Hampton. 'Twill be an excellent match and they'll be living here at Belvoir. But it will be well for George William to have a firsthand look at the family holdings since eventually he will inherit much of them."

George thought of the Ferry Farm property that would be his. A scrubby, insignificant legacy compared with these magnificent lands along the Potomac. "I must make my own future," he thought. Idly he wondered about George William's future bride. Sally Carey must indeed have many attributes if she had conquered the selective heart of the scion of the Fairfax family.

A PPLAUSE FILLED THE CHAMBER AGAIN. This time it was a tribute to the ideals and hopes the President-elect had offered to his country in his Inaugural Address.

Then Chief Justice Oliver Ellsworth came forth to administer the oath of office. Slowly Adams repeated after the Justice . . . "I, John Adams, do solemnly swear that I will support the Constitution of the United States."

Now the chamber hall was silent. Crammed so that it would have been impossible for one more human being to press into it, the words, shyly spoken, echoed throughout. "I, John Adams, do solemnly swear . . ."

The tightness of a facial muscle, the brightness in an eye, the quivering of a nostril—nearly every face betrayed deep emotion, sadness as well as pride.

But George's countenance was serene and unclouded as he listened to the words that took the mantle of the Presidency from him and rested it on another man. He had wondered about this moment, about how he would feel. He had even feared that he might have a terrible sense of finality even though he badly wanted the release.

But instead he experienced only pride—pride at the events that had led his country to this moment, pride at the orderly transition of government, pride at the continuity of the infant nation.

He thought of the cloying heat of that summer ten years ago when he and some fifty-five other delegates had gathered in this city to recast the Articles of Confederation and to consider the state of the union. Somehow during that summer a miracle had taken place.

The representatives of thirteen states had come here jealously guarding their individual prerogatives, fearing and mistrusting each other. And somehow, after they had closed the shutters against street noise and the incessant flies, they had managed to ignore the discomfort of the airless, hot room and put themselves to the awesome task before them.

They had debated and argued, adopted unmovable stands and then compromised, despaired and found new hope, until in the end they had achieved the stunning document that John Adams was now swearing to defend.

Eight years before, George had been painfully aware that many of his own actions would set precedents for his successors to follow. In a way he had charted the course of the Presidency as he had once charted a wilderness in Virginia. So long ago . . . so very long ago . . . nearly five decades now.

John Adams was swearing to defend the Constitution of the United States, but George was listening to the cultured voice of George William Fairfax as they began their month-long expedition into the wilderness.

THE EXPEDITION WAS UNDER THE SUPERvision of James Genn, an experienced surveyor. George made a number of attempts to become friendly with the man but found him brusque and taciturn. Genn also seemed thoroughly awed by George William Fairfax, and never addressed him without stringing his sentence with phrases like "if you please, sir," "as it pleases you, sir." At the end of the day Genn would quickly go to where his helpers were gathered, even though he could have elected to spend his rest periods with George William and George.

As a result George and George William were thrown together for company. George quickly got over his shyness with the young heir and just as quickly stopped calling him "Mr. Fairfax." By the time they'd passed Powell's Creek on the third day, they were on an easy first-name basis and the seeds of a lifelong friendship had been sown.

Actually, George knew that he had no reason not to be at ease with George William. Ferry Farm might not have the grandeur of Belvoir but he *was* a gentleman's son and had a gentleman's desire for a comfortable bed and good food. After a hard day's riding he was able to deplore some of the vermin-infested lodgings with as much disdain as his sophisticated companion.

On some of the evenings George William told him about his fiancée. "You'll not believe how lovely she is until you see her. Dark hair and flashing eyes and the slimness of a sprite. And quick-witted—my God, how I hate a woman without a mind. Thanks to her father's training Sally is probably better informed than most of our men, and I include the Harvard graduates. She dances like an angel and there I confess she leaves me behind. This blasted rheumatism doesn't suit itself to the ballroom."

He spoke lightly about the rheumatism as he did about everything, but it was a very real ailment. On damp mornings he'd get up rubbing his knees and grimacing as he moved. After a while the stiffness worked out but it always returned.

George admired the way his companion dismissed the discomfort as being unworthy of discussion. He admired equally the way young Fairfax always managed to look fastidious even in the comparatively plain clothes that he wore during the expedition. George found himself increasingly anxious to meet the much-praised Sally.

After the trip was over he went back to Ferry Farm.

The thirty-two days had convinced him of his liking for the surveyor's occupation and he began working in earnest, even applying for a license to William and Mary College. Inwardly he felt restless and driven. He wanted to do everything, know everything. He frequently took long rides by himself, carefully examining his own emotions. What was the cause of his dissatisfaction? Nothing . . . everything.

He simply wasn't happy at Ferry Farm. His mother was a grossly untidy housekeeper and it set his teeth on edge to see the chaos of the house, the haphazard service at the table. He disliked the plain, poorly sewn clothing she had made for him. He felt inadequate at social gatherings, probably because he danced poorly and knew none of the fashionable games. There was no merriment or games at home.

Resolutely he set about correcting what he could. With his first earnings he ordered new shirts and new waistcoats. George acknowledged to himself that he had two models now. He still wanted to be like Lawrence but Lawrence was quiet. It had become important to acquire some of the easy grace of George William.

The next step was to prevail on some of his numerous young cousins to teach him whist and loo. He found the games boring but deliberately practiced until he became accomplished in them.

It was months after the expedition before he returned to Mount Vernon. When he rode up the familiar path, he had a sense of having passed a certain barrier. This time money he had earned was jingling in his pocket; this time he was wearing clothing of his own selection. He grinned to himself. This time he probably wouldn't even trip over his own feet.

As usual Mount Vernon seemed to reach out to greet him. It was dusk when he arrived and lights still shone in all the downstairs rooms. A roaring fire licked hungrily in the hearth and Lawrence had a decanter of wine waiting.

The brothers greeted each other enthusiastically, and Lawrence praised George's appearance, even before bringing him to the bedroom to see Anne, who had given birth to a new baby girl.

George kissed his sister-in-law affectionately. She was always so kind to him and had that air of careless grace that so intrigued him in the entire Fairfax family. She proudly showed off the new baby, a beautiful flower-like infant. But even to George's unskilled eyes, the baby seemed frail.

It was as though Anne could read his thoughts. "She looks so tiny but I know she's sturdier than the others." Her voice was a plea for reassurance.

George gingerly held a finger out and the baby closed her fist over it. "She has a fine grasp," he remarked, and it was the right thing to say. Anne smiled happily.

The next day, at Lawrence's suggestion, they rode over to Belvoir so that George could meet George William's bride, Sally. The wedding had taken place several months earlier.

George selected what he considered the finest of the waistcoats, collars, and shirts and dressed carefully. But when he and Lawrence rode up the tree-shaded path that led to the main entrance of the magnificent brick mansion, he felt strangely awkward and shy. Suppose George William's bride didn't like him. Suppose she considered him callow and uninteresting. He repressed a desire to give a tug to his reins and send his horse back in the direction of Mount Vernon. Instead he dismounted, surrendered the animal to a groom, and, at Lawrence's side, mounted the steps of the wide veranda.

George William must have seen them approaching because he came to open the door himself, smiling his welcome. "You cut a finer figure than you did on the trail," he told George, laughing.

George nodded in self-conscious admission of his new clothes.

And then *she* came. Down the winding staircase, her footstep light and with one slim hand holding the banister. She was wearing a white gown with a green bodice, and the green seemed to be exactly the shade of her eyes. Her dark hair was piled softly on her head except for the cluster of curls at the nape of her neck. She smiled adoringly at George William, then turned to Lawrence. "So at last you have brought your brother to meet me," she said.

She extended both hands to George. "I've heard so much about you."

I've heard so much about you. George was stunned. My God, the unbelievable beauty of her—the sparkle in her eyes—the slimness. He felt too tall, too broad. He was flustered and confused and shy and at the same time completely at home. "I can't imagine why, ma'am," he stammered.

She shook her head in mock severity. "That's no kind of answer," she told him. "It's very important to have a sense of your own worth. My husband tells me you ride your horse with the skill of an Indian. You have the instincts of a great surveyor. You have a writer's ability to keep a journal. You're an excellent accountant. He even said that you swear like a sailor at bad accommodations."

George felt himself blushing furiously. "I assure you, ma'am . . ."

She smiled. "Now you're not supposed to apologize. I meant it as a compliment. But in conclusion George William has already told me that you have the mark of greatness on you, and I trust his judgment."

"Madame," George said, "if his selection of a wife is the measure of his judgment, I would trust my future to him implicitly."

Lawrence and George William burst into laughter. "You see my brother is growing up rapidly," Lawrence said.

George William nodded. "I shall have to keep a stern eye on Sally's sisters when they come to visit."

George did not bother to correct his friend. He realized that he was still holding Sally's hands. She gently withdrew them but he knew that from that moment on he'd never be the same. What did it matter what her sisters were like? What *any* young woman was like was of no importance.

Sally was two years older than he. She was married to his good friend. She was forever unattainable.

And he was in love with her.

IT WAS A COLD, BLEAK MARCH MORNING and the English resort of Bath was gray and misty in the early morning fog. Sally Carey Fairfax awakened slowly with the knowledge that soon she would pick up the burden that had been mercifully lifted while she slept. In a moment she would come to the full realization that she was alone. George William had been dead for months, but for an instant before full awakening she could still pretend he was with her.

Or better still she could pretend that they were all young again, all at the beginning. She sighed and turned her face so that the pillow brushed away the tear that slipped down her cheek. Her body, so slender in youth, was now too thin. The flawless complexion that had been the envy of her friends had become finely lined, the thick black hair was now completely white under her nightcap.

Before she slept she'd been reading the paper and it had announced that a new President was being inaugurated in the former Colonies—the United States of America. The paper had announced that the first President, George Washington, would be leaving public office at noon.

Sally opened her eyes long enough to glance at the clock ticking on the mantel. That was *now*. At this moment at home a new President was being sworn in.

Now he would be going back to Mount Vernon. She smiled unconsciously as she thought of the gentle sweep of the Virginia countryside. She thought of how she and George William had raced their horses across the land between Belvoir and Mount Vernon to collect young George for the hunt. She remembered the evenings they'd all spent together by the fire, planning their futures, discussing the future of Virginia and the Colonies.

Oh, those were the happy years, she thought, the happiest years, the ones that began when as a bride of eighteen she'd been mistress of Belvoir and George had lived with Lawrence and Anne at Mount Vernon.

She could still remember his shyness, his awkward movements, and then the unexpected grace he'd shown when she insisted on teaching him to dance. Already touched with the rheumatism that was to scourge him, her young husband had smilingly declined to join them but had watched with warm approval as she and George tried the steps in the ballroom.

Even then young George had had that something, that special mark that promised what he would become. "It's a good thing I loved my husband so," Sally thought. "If I had loved him less . . ."

Tears welled in her eyes. She and George William had talked about going back to Virginia but Belvoir had been ruined during the war.

She laid her hand on the empty pillow beside her. But her thoughts were not so much of the husband she had so recently lost as of the man who right now was participating in a ceremony in Philadelphia.

Was he still as straight as when he rode over the plantation with her? Was he still courtly? Had he given up dancing yet?

Dear God, how she had loved to dance with him.

What was he like now? . . .

THE TRAGEDY THAT HAD SHADOWED Anne and Lawrence would not depart. The baby still kept a grip on life but was extremely delicate. It was obvious to everyone, except perhaps Lawrence and Anne, that this baby would not survive much longer than her predecessors.

And as Lawrence and Anne hovered anxiously over her cradle, another cross came. The hard, racking cough that had plagued Lawrence for nearly three years had worsened. He lost weight steadily and the doctors feared that he would not last in the damp winter climate. He was told to leave immediately for the West Indies.

It was unthinkable that Anne could leave her child, so George volunteered to accompany his sick brother.

George went to Belvoir to say good-bye to Sally and George William. The concern in their faces both comforted and saddened him. "It is a hopeless journey," he said bluntly.

George William poured the wine carefully. "I'm afraid so."

"Take care of Anne and the baby and Mount Vernon. I don't know how long I'll be gone." He put his glass down and walked over to the window, embarrassed by the emotion he knew was in his face.

Then Sally's soft hand was on his arm. "It's very hard for you."

"Yes . . . Lawrence has been . . . since my father died . . ."

"No matter what happens, you'll still belong here."

Would he, he wondered, would he? How much of the Fairfax kindness was for him alone? How much because he was Lawrence's brother and Lawrence's wife was a Fairfax? Would he always lose the people who were dearest to him?

He became aware of the hand on his arm. Or never have the one who was dearest of all?

In bleak misery he turned away and started to leave.

George William stopped him. "You're staying for dinner. It's not to be discussed."

Sally's servants were well-trained. The dinner was hot, bountiful, the mutton properly seasoned, the wines delicate and light. George William easily kept the conversation on the crops, the assembly, the governor, the looming trouble with the French over the forts along the Ohio.

Finally, over coffee he seemed to take measure of the more relaxed mood of his guest and spoke bluntly.

"My dear friend, I think that we must all realize that Lawrence's days are numbered. If what we fear should happen, I think it best that Anne come home here with her baby. Mount Vernon needs a master's hand and would be impossible to run alone. But it needs to be run. And it will fall to you to do the job."

Mount Vernon . . . somehow he'd never thought of it as anything but Lawrence's home. "I want Lawrence to live to be master of Mount Vernon," he said stubbornly.

"George, be honest. It's not like you not to face the truth. It may look unseemly even to discuss this now but I think you will need courage in the days ahead. It is you who will have to watch Lawrence fail. In those dark days that are coming, try to think of the future. Try to think that one day you will be back with us, in your place near us—and your place is Mount Vernon."

For the first time since the realization of Lawrence's fate had sunk in, he felt a measure of surcease. Would he always draw his strength from that land and that house, which was really so small compared with the one in which he now sat?

But an hour later, when he left, after George William's firm handclasp and Sally's sisterly kiss on his cheek, he knew he had the strength for whatever the immediate future brought.

And he had need for that strength. The boat journey was long and immensely tiring to Lawrence. To George it was exhilarating to stand on the deck and watch the sailors at work—to see the variety of tasks and to muse over what his own life would have been if he'd been allowed to go to sea. He confessed to himself that he no longer regretted the fact that he hadn't gone.

Barbados was warm, cheerful, and brilliantly colorful. Lawrence seemed to revive somewhat and even accepted an invitation to dinner from an old friend, Major Clarke, whom he'd met at Cartagena.

The evening with Major Clarke had a lifelong effect on George. When he and Lawrence arrived for dinner, the major apologized for the fact that his family would not be able to join them at the table, saying casually that his daughter was suffering from smallpox. The news made George somewhat apprehensive but Lawrence didn't seem to mind and the evening turned into a very pleasant one.

The following week George himself was far from well and was grateful that, for the time at least, Lawrence seemed to be in good spirits and coughing less. Then exactly fourteen days after the dinner at Major Clarke's George awoke with a raging fever and desperately sore throat. Even before the doctor came, he knew he'd somehow contracted the smallpox.

For days he was critically ill. Then as the fever slowly abated, he came to realize that he'd be marked with ugly pustule scars for the rest of his life.

George tried not to let it matter, but Lawrence noticed and commented on his depression. "You may yet thank the day that you've had this blasted pox," Lawrence told him. "Certainly if you should join the militia and ever see service for His Majesty, you'll be considered one of the lucky ones. The pox is a scourge to any army and those who have immunity don't mind bearing a few beauty marks."

"Hardly beauty marks," George said wryly, and was glad he wasn't home. He missed Sally with an ache that seemed a part of his very being but was vain enough to be grateful that she couldn't see him while the scars were still so raw and deep.

Then he forgot them because the first promise of Lawrence's rally soon began to fade. The coughing became incessant. The little weight he'd gained vanished.

Finally, one night, George woke to find his brother

standing over his bed, clutching at the headboard. He jumped up in alarm. Quickly he made Lawrence lie on the bed, propped him against the pillows, and brought water to him. "You'll be better in the morning."

Lawrence shook his head weakly. "It's no use, George. I'd hoped, really hoped . . . Some people can lick this but I can't. George, I want to see Anne. I don't want to die without seeing her again. Will you go home and get her for me? Sally will take care of the baby—I know she will—George, go home and get Anne."

He'd expected that he wouldn't see Virginia for at least a year, but four months after his departure he was going home again. Lawrence's words of farewell unwittingly touched a sore spot. "It's such a long journey and you're not well yourself, but someday, when you fall in love, you'll understand how desperately I need to be with Anne now."

When he fell in love . . . For hours he stood on the deck of the ship on the return voyage, staring unseeingly at the horizon.

Anne was staying at Belvoir and he went there as soon as he got home. As gently as he could he told her that Lawrence wanted her to join him. Anne took the news bravely. "My husband is not going to get well." The words were more statement than question. She did not wait for an answer but said, "George, take me to him at once, please. Sally, you'll watch the baby."

George hadn't had a chance to do more than glance at Sally. Anne had met him at the door with anxious questions.

Now he turned to her, full face, and her expression of shocked concern was balm to his spirit. Swiftly she came to his side and ran her fingertips over his face. "You've had such a bad time." Then she looked at Anne. "Of course I'll mind the baby. High time I had some practice."

It was the first time George ever heard her refer to the fact that after a year of marriage she was not yet with child. Then he forgot even her in his concern for the sadness in Anne's face.

"Are you really strong enough to accompany me, George?" she asked him. "We did you little favor in asking you to make the first journey."

"I'm completely strong," he assured her. "You can count on me always."

George William immediately began making arrangements for the return trip but then word came from Lawrence. "I cannot wait for you to come. And it is useless for me to stay here. I'm coming home to you. If I must die, I want to be with my loved ones. I want to be in my home and see the face of my little one again."

The homecoming was a sad one. The shadow of death hovered over Lawrence's gaunt, gray face, his thin body. Even his magnificent carriage seemed stooped now from the endless coughing bouts. He had little more than a month. He had the lovely Virginia spring and the warmth of the sun on his shoulders as he sat through golden afternoons with Anne and the baby on the lawn overlooking the river.

Often he talked to George about the future. "You have a head on your shoulders. You will do well. Never be afraid. I rather wish that I could be here to see you progress. Somehow I think Sally is right and that the world shall hear much of you. Now, let me give you a few ideas of what I think you should do."

During those months George lost any fear of death that he'd ever had. He watched Lawrence's quiet acceptance of the Divine Plan, the facing up by the dying man to what the future would hold for his family, the wisdom with which he saw that future.

"Eventually be a candidate for the House of Burgesses," he counseled. "It's necessary for a man to help in forming the laws by which he must live. Someday Mount Vernon will be yours. I hope and wish that Anne will marry again."

The end came in July. George and Anne were with Lawrence and could not begrudge his death. It was a relief to see the peace return to the strained and tortured face. Several months after the funeral Anne told George that she was going to live at Belvoir with the baby. Lawrence had left the house to Anne and the baby with George as residuary heir. By now it was obvious that the baby would soon follow her father and her share of Mount Vernon would belong to George.

It was obvious too that Anne meant it when she asked George to make Mount Vernon his home. "Someday it will belong to you," she said calmly. "Please take care of it now."

"But will you be happy leaving it?" George asked.

"Happy?" For a moment the patrician calm left Anne's face. "What is happiness? I have known so much sorrow in this house, yet so much joy, too. I could never live here. There is a life waiting for me, I think, but I will not find it in these walls."

And so he was alone in Mount Vernon with only the servants for company. For weeks George wandered through the house, unseeingly. Days he cast all his energy into surveying, but at night he was often too weary even for sleep and would restlessly pace the downstairs floor until dawn.

But then the winter passed and spring came again. As his heart lightened he began to look at his home with a proprietor's eye. The way it compared with Belvoir displeased him mightily. There was so much to do, so very much. He began making a list of the first furnishings he would order and a plan of the necessary carpentry and mason work. He didn't even suspect that he was beginning a task that would give him a major amount of the pleasure of his lifetime. It was then, and always would be, a labor of love.

Socially he began to venture out more. That spring was gay with balls and foxhunting. George could ride with the finest although he had little taste for the kill.

At the dances . . . well, he'd had a good teacher. Sally always chose to try the new steps with him. George William's rheumatism was increasing steadily and he cheerfully relinquished the opportunity of practicing with his wife. "For heaven's sake, let an old man sit in the corner and talk about our crotchety governor," he would laugh. "George, be a good friend and try the new steps with Sally."

For a time he was stiff and shy. His mother had spent little money on dancing masters for her offspring. But then the native grace and rhythm which made him at home on a mount came to his rescue and he realized that dancing came very naturally. Finally it was Sally who, flushed and breathless, would say, "Dear Lord, young Washington, the pupil has surpassed the teacher. Take Mary for your partner and let me sit with my husband."

Mary Carey, Sally's sister, was so like Sally. For a time George wondered if it were possible that after all he would find happiness with someone who wasn't Sally but so nearly resembled her. He tried. For a time he lounged on the floor by her chair during evenings at Belvoir. For a time he rode at her side during the hunts.

Then, one evening at a ball at Belvoir, while they were dancing together, he hesitantly suggested that Mount Vernon had need of a mistress.

The remark made Mary turn stony-faced. The music ended as she said, "And I have need of a man who loves me well." She turned on her heel and walked away from him.

George stood staring perplexed until he felt a hand on his arm. "Whatever is the matter?" Sally asked.

The moment of disappointment passed immediately. "I think, madame, I have just been refused as a potential suitor."

Sally smiled. "I think, young Washington, that if you wish to court my sister, you must act rather more in love, and less like a man who is thinking of adding to his possessions. I would have thought that teaching you to dance was enough. Must I also teach you how to love?"

The remark had started out to be a light one. But suddenly Sally blushed crimson. The music began and George bowed low. "May I have the honor?"

Lightly she accepted his arm and they took their

places on the floor. The telltale blush had made him reckless. "Do you really think it necessary to teach me how to love," he demanded, "or don't you think you've taught me too well? Sally, oh Sally . . ."

"I'm not sure I know you very well at the moment." Her voice was still breathless and unsure. "You seem quite different and I'm not sure I like the change."

He steered her off the floor. Recklessly he took her arm and started to propel her toward the east door. But suddenly George William was standing in front of them and without his usually genial smile. His glance at Sally was a request for explanation.

Easily she smiled at him. "I have just learned that our good friend and neighbor is not to be our brother-in-law."

George William's expression became relieved, then sympathetic. "So that's it. I'm sorry, of course. Mary is a fine girl—like her sister." He looked full into his wife's face. "No, not completely like her. There isn't anyone like Sally."

George looked at her, too. The moment of recklessness had passed and he was aghast at his own near folly. If George William hadn't come along, he'd be outside with Sally now and she would be in his arms. He'd been an instant away from violating all the friendship and trust the Fairfaxes had shown him.

The musicians were still playing and George William took Sally's arm. "I can manage this with you, my dear."

George stood aside as they passed, then went outside and ordered his horse brought around. As he waited he bleakly echoed George William's words: "There isn't anyone like Sally."

A ND WILL, TO THE BEST OF MY ABILITY, preserve, protect, and defend the Constitution of the United States."

. . . It seemed that even the colorless voice of John Adams assumed majesty with the swearing of the solemn oath. The applause this time was subdued but fervent and the attitude of the assemblage seemed almost prayerful.

Adams returned to his seat. Then rose again and the second President of the United States strode from the hall.

George watched him go. He'd wanted to congratulate him but the departure had been too quick. He felt a quick flash of irritation. It would have been more seemly for the man to have waited, to have permitted felicitations.

But that was John Adams for you.

George sighed. He would do the only thing possible . . . walk over to the Francis Hotel where Adams was lodging and offer his congratulations immediately.

Adams in his gilded coach would be there in a minute.

But George rather liked the walk. A sense of freedom swept through him. He was a private citizen now. There'd be no following, no interest in his movements. As a private citizen he'd congratulate the new President and then go back to Patsy.

Tonight there was the reception for him in the amphitheater but tomorrow, first thing, they'd begin dismantling the house and getting it ready for the Adams family.

He stirred restively. Why wasn't Jefferson taking his leave? Good heavens, the man was gesturing for him to go. Absolutely improper. The Vice President followed the chief executive. No private citizen preceded him.

He shook his head. Jefferson continued to signal his wish that George begin the recessional.

George shook his head again. Thomas must take precedence. It was a matter of respect to the government, not of friendship.

Reluctantly the tall blue-coated figure started toward the door at the far end of the chamber. After he was halfway down the room, George left his own seat.

He found his exit blocked. The crowds thronged around him. There were sounds of scuffling feet and excited chatter but it seemed to him a curious silence somehow pervaded each spot he passed. It seemed that the people were taking his measure, were judging him.

In public office he'd schooled himself to do what he thought was best and to not be swayed by public comment—either praise or blame.

He reached the door and turned briskly down the north side of Chestnut Street. Vaguely he was aware that Timothy Pickering was walking beside him. But he didn't engage him in conversation. He wanted to think.

What kind of job had he done?

Suddenly it was like the time that he'd returned from the Braddock campaign, tortured, with self-doubt—when he was first an officer in the militia.

He brushed a piece of lint from his black velvet jacket.

The black velvet was a far cry from the first uniform . . . that blue coat, faced and cuffed with scarlet and trimmed with silver. The scarlet waistcoat and silver lace . . . the silver-laced hat and blue breeches.

Oh, he'd cut a fine figure of a soldier, or so he had thought—and all this before he'd ever been exposed to what soldiering was.

He glanced back a moment. A crowd had begun to follow him. In heaven's name why?

He was at the end . . . not the beginning.

He'd been decommissioned now. For good.

Remember the thrill of that first commission?

It had been after Lawrence died. And after something else.

Of course.

It was after the realization came that he had somehow to make a life that didn't include a hopeless dream of Sally. That was when the appointment had come. The governor had announced that he was to take Lawrence's place as District Adjutant of His Majesty's Colony of Virginia and he'd been designated a major in the Colonial Corps.

A major . . . before he'd ever tried his hand at soldiering.

He'd fancied himself as cutting a fine figure in his regimental dress but maybe at twenty-one that was forgivable.

And he had worked hard. He'd taken fencing and drilled for hours. He'd disciplined himself for active service.

The Francis Hotel was just down the block. He was almost there.

John Adams was beginning a four-year term.

How long had he served in the regiment the first time? Between '53 and '55. And then he'd resigned because of the eternal wrangling over the chain of command. A Colonial commission meant nothing if a British Regular came on the scene in those days. He'd resigned the commission and gone home to a Mount Vernon that was completely his. The baby was dead and Anne had remarried. He had taken over her inheritance in the property. The house had been forlorn and neglected so he'd begun ordering tools and stock and furnishings.

This time he'd be going home with Patsy.

He arrived at the tavern and went inside. But then he stood uncertainly at the staircase. So many people had followed him. It seemed churlish to ignore them. Perhaps he should speak to them . . .

Not quite knowing what he would say, he reached slowly for the knob and pulled the door open.

The people waiting outside were still silent, but every face shouted love and compassion. He stared at them for a long moment. For these, at least, there was no jubilee in the ending of his administration.

Blinding tears came to his eyes. Quickly he turned and went inside. This time he didn't hesitate but began to climb the stairs resolutely.

It was time to call on his superior, the President of the United States.

Just as, long ago, he had first paid his respects to Braddock.

E STILL SPENT MUCH TIME AT BELVOIR but the nearly two years of service had done much to mature him. At twenty-three he was not the same reckless fool who within five minutes had proposed to one sister and tried to make love to the other.

He could sit by the hour in Belvoir now, talking with George William, discussing the worsening situation with the French at the Ohio; the coming of General Braddock to lead the English and Colonial forces; the plight of the settlers in the Ohio region.

Impulsively he'd written a letter to General Braddock welcoming him to the Colonies and congratulating him on his assignment. Somewhat hesitantly he admitted that fact to George William.

His friend's eyebrows shot up. "So you've taken to writing letters of welcome to visiting military royalty."

George flushed. "I merely wished—"

George William interrupted. "You merely wished the general to say to Governor Dinwiddie, 'And who is this

Washington?' At which point the governor would say, 'Damned fine soldier and insolent enough to resign rather than not have clear command.' At that point the general, who badly needs good officers, would be intrigued and inquire more—isn't that what you hope?"

"No such thing." But he knew that his tone lacked conviction.

Sally was bent over her sewing, a slight frown on her forehead. George had often thought that she was the only woman he knew who looked more at home with a book in her hand than a piece of embroidery.

"My feeling," she began with emphasis.

Both men looked at her, smiling.

"The last time you had a feeling, I found myself ordering a new carriage because your feeling was that the present one was shabby. Out with it, my love, but remember it's been an ill year for tobacco." George William's tone was indulgent.

Sally assumed an air of great dignity. "This has nothing to do with any purchases. I was about to say that my feeling has always been that our neighbor, here present, is well suited to military life and that much will be heard of him in that field. Don't ask me why . . . it's just . . ."

"A feeling," George finished for her. "George William, your lovely wife is a dreamer."

George William tapped his pipe against the fire-place. When he answered his voice was thoughtful. "Do you know, I'm as sure that she's right about this as I was that she'd have her new carriage when she started insulting the old one."

They all laughed and the subject was dropped, but the next day when George returned to the house after an inspection tour with his overseer, he found a letter awaiting him. It was an invitation from General Braddock to join the campaign against the French and an assurance that any question of regulation of command could be settled.

For a long time he paced the downstairs rooms. Did he or did he not want this invitation? There was so much to do at home. Both inside and out the plantation clearly showed the effects of his absence during the last military campaign. He'd agreed to buy Anne's share of Mount Vernon and needed financing. The house needed work. These military campaigns could drag on for years. There was nothing to compel him to go. Then why was he even considering it?

He was considering—no, *deciding* to go because he was needed. Because he, more than most men, understood the value of the magnificent land along the Ohio. If the French were allowed to erect forts and seize that land, England and the Colonies would be permitting a priceless heritage to slip through their fingers. Future colonists would need to push westward. It was vital that their progress should not be stopped by French guns. George knew that when General Braddock came to Virginia, he would join his party.

He did make one concession to his responsibilities at Mount Vernon. He decided to go with the general as a volunteer officer without pay. Then he would be free to return home after a year if matters on the plantation necessitated his presence.

His mother heard of the decision and hastened to Mount Vernon. The scene was similar to when she'd forbidden him to go to sea but with one essential difference. He was twenty-three now, not sixteen. He was master of his own home and he had the right to his own life.

He fought her rage but not with angry words, although they crowded his throat, begging for utterance. Instead he showed her exquisite courtesy which only infuriated her the more.

"I'll not have it! Nonsense! Stay home where you belong. Your brother Lawrence would be alive now if he hadn't gone on that fool campaign and returned with no lungs in his body. And who will take care of this place?" His mother's voice seemed even shriller as she got older.

"Jack will, I hope." His younger brother, John Augustine, had accompanied their mother on the visit.

"Jack, could you tear yourself away from Ferry Farm and stay here till my return? If Mother can spare you, of course."

Jack said quickly, "Mother finds me of little use at Ferry Farm. Oh, yes . . . yes, George, I'll gladly stay here."

George looked at his tall young brother with wry affection. Lawrence had given him a home—a refuge from his mother. Now he was doing the same thing for Jack. Then he sighed as his mother stalked angrily from the room. For a man who daily felt an increasing need for a woman to share his life, he realized that he was not very grateful for the one woman he had.

He soon discovered that there would be as much frustration in this campaign as there had been in the last one. Braddock might be a brilliant commander but, as George realized almost immediately, he was not prepared to surrender his established notions of proper military warfare. Accordingly, George's suggestions to pack animals rather than wagons with supplies, so that the army could move quickly and easily, fell on deaf ears.

At the conferences in Braddock's quarters George tried tactfully to point out that fighting Indians who could slide away in the woods was quite different from meeting another army in full dress on an open plain. At first the general seemed to be listening to his suggestions but it soon became obvious that he did not take them seriously. He was clearly about to recover Fort Duquesne in his own way.

George could feel his blood heat even while he kept his manner courteous and his face impassive. He had a clear picture of the kind of target the British Regulars would make in their bright jackets. He knew too that Braddock was not maintaining a consistent policy with the friendly Indians. He did not suspect that one day, as commander in chief of a revolution, he would bless the British for their shortsightedness in both these areas.

The responsibility for assembling the supplies fell to him. He frequently told himself that he'd rather face the entire French Army with a dozen soldiers behind him than work on the near-hopeless task of properly equipping an army. Money was short; horses were promised but not delivered; meat arrived from contractors in such vile state that he ordered it buried; shipments of flour did not arrive. The trails were so bad that the overloaded wagons collapsed.

But at last they were ready for the march. George was bone weary but anxious to get into action. He had volunteered his services because he wanted to serve his country and King. Certainly he'd never anticipated spending weeks and months arguing the price of flour with traders who more properly could be called robbers.

Then, just as the march was to begin, he contracted the bloody flux that had swept through the camp. He'd thought he was immune, that his strong body could cast off any germs, but he was no match for this ailment. Feebly he damned his luck as, abed with fever and weakness, he watched the troops leave the camp.

Braddock, considerately enough, stopped to wish him well before leaving. George did manage to wring a promise from the commander. If he could recover sufficiently, he could join the regiment and be present when the fort was retaken.

The camp seemed desolate and quiet after the main force was gone. He could not seem to shake the paralyzing weakness which left him somber and depressed. Loneliness added to his miseries. There was little communication and at one point he wrote John Augustine, sarcastically bidding him to thank his friends for the letters they hadn't sent.

After that letter was mailed, he felt twice as wretched. He'd meant Sally, of course. But she had written several times. And what more could he expect. As the fever swept over him again, he knew that what he wanted of her in time and thought and attention could only be required of a wife.

Gradually the weakness left and he began to recover.

Over the strenuous objections of the doctor he declared himself well enough to catch up with the general's staff. He was frantic with anxiety now. An advanced column had been sent and all indications were that the move to take the fort before the French could get new supplies would go well.

George allowed one concession to his illness. When his horse was being saddled he permitted cushions to be put between the saddle and the animal's body to protect his aching body from the jolting of the ride.

The unseasonable heat in Pennsylvania was distressing to him and he blamed the weather for his inability to share the lighthearted sense of conquest that Braddock and his staff exhibited when he caught up with them. They reported that the advance column had encountered no opposition, not even scouts. Why, undoubtedly, they'd take Duquesne in a few hours.

The day they began to cross the Monongahela River was July 9. George felt the quickening of his senses as they began this last leg before the battle site.

There was an exultation coursing through him similar to what he felt when he was at home in Mount Vernon. Oh, granted, he didn't feel this way all the time on a military campaign, certainly not when he was cooling his heels for weeks in dismal little towns, trying frantically to get supplies. He stretched his shoulders back, totally unaware of what an imposing figure he was to the men around him.

Actually he would have been surprised to know how blindly his men loved and trusted him. He even felt that his air of reserve which had begun in his mother's household was a detriment to him in his relationship with the troops. He'd heard himself termed "haughty" and felt the word unfair but could do nothing to alter it. He shrugged inwardly and gave the command to cross the river.

The forging of Turtle Creek was simple, but a warning bell seemed to clang in his mind. He pointed out to General Braddock that the riverbank was muddy with the signs of many feet. The general's barely concealed impatience made George wheel his horse back into the line of march.

He'd been here on the last campaign, nineteen months before. The weather had been bitterly cold then, but now the trees were thick and green, the foliage dense.

He didn't like it.

There was a clearing near Fraser's Trading Post. They were still a day's march from the fort. If he were the French commander, he would not let an enemy get much closer. He would find a place to stage an ambush.

Where better than right here where the troops were regrouping from the water crossing, where the forest gave coverage to an attacker?

Where better . . .

The roll of a volley shattered the precise sound of the military marching. George reined his horse in sharply. Heavy fire was followed by another volley. Then the sound he'd been waiting for came. An Indian war whoop split the air.

The battle had begun.

George realized afterward that he could never really reconstruct the hours that ensued. He simply followed his instincts.

Afterward he listened in amazement as his fellow officers cited him for "the greatest courage and resolution."

Afterward he found the four bullet holes through his uniform coat. Afterward he was able to grieve for the horse that was shot out from under him.

An aide came to him with the word that General Braddock had been wounded. Somehow he managed to procure a wagon and get the dying commander across the river.

Braddock remained lucid to the end. He gave orders calmly and even told George he wanted him to have his own horse and his body servant, Bishop. He died only sensing how enormous the disaster had been. He died without knowledge of the screams of the wounded as they were scalped, of the prisoners as they were burned at stakes.

It fell to George to regroup the remnants of the British and Colonial forces, to give the orders to fall back. But first he had one mission to perform for General Braddock.

As his fellow officers watched in amazement, he chose the site of the general's burial. The trench was dug in the very road over which the column would pass. The hundreds of horses hooves would assure that no sign would remain of the grave where a brave and stubborn general was resting.

Captain Dobson asked why this was necessary. George asked him in return if he'd ever seen a body discovered and dishonored by the Indians.

The retreat was accomplished and then he was free to go home. Another campaign would have to be formed, another attempt made. It was not only the issue of the forts now. It was the prestige of Britain and her Colonies, but first plans would have to be made. Men would have to be recruited.

Wearily George began the long trip to Mount Vernon. He was heavyhearted and discouraged. He blamed himself for his part in the failure.

He did not see the worshiping glances of the troops who were still at camp when he rode away. He did not yet know that all Virginia was telling the tale of his bravery.

He did not even consider the significance of the fact that he was riding the dead general's horse and attended by the dead general's servant.

He did not sense that the mantle of leadership had settled firmly on his shoulders.

THE FIRE BLAZED WARM AND HEARTEN-
ing in the small study, but outside a frigid
wind beat against the casements. Patsy sat by the window
and peered anxiously into the street. Her eyes searched
the long block looking for the tall figure who should be
coming now.

Surely the ceremony was completed. Surely he
should be on the way home.

She wished he had let her go with him. It was all well
enough to be glad to be finished with the Presidency, but
no one could fail to have some regrets at stepping aside
when the actual moment came.

And she knew that some of the newspaper articles
had wounded and disturbed him. He'd be wondering how
many shared that editor's feelings about the ending of his
administration.

Where was he? He should have taken the carriage
instead of walking on such a windy day. He had to start

realizing that he wasn't as strong as he used to be and that his throat flared up whenever he was chilled.

Resolutely she picked up her needlework. Foolish, foolish to worry so much. He was probably just visiting with Adams or Jefferson.

But he needed to rest. Tonight they would be up late at the reception.

How many times in these forty years had she waited for him, worried about him. She could still feel the clammy fear that used to haunt her when he was away at the front during the war. People ran to her with news of the general's daring and bravery . . .

From the time he'd survived the massacre at Monongahela there'd been a legend that he couldn't be wounded in battle.

Small comfort that legend had been in the nights when she lay awake wondering if he'd live to come back to her.

Was that . . .

Yes, it was. Far down the street a tall figure was approaching.

He seemed to be leaning forward a little, bracing himself against the wind.

As she watched, his pace quickened.

He was hurrying now.

An upsurge of relief and lightheartedness surged

through her. Unheeded, her needlework slipped to the carpet. After forty years her heart still beat faster when he came.

Forty years . . . a lifetime ago . . . Her heart had pounded when her husband, Daniel Custis, had drawn her forward to be introduced to the hero of the Monongahela campaign.

He had seemed like a young god to her then with his great height and breadth accentuated by his blue-and-silver uniform and the courtly reserve in his manner

And now the white-haired, black-clad, slightly stooped figure was almost to the house.

Patsy hurried across the room and down the stairs to let her general in.

It was August when he arrived home. As usual the land restored both his body and spirits. George found that his strength returned quickly as once again he took the reins of his establishment into his own hands. Days he rode on the grounds, supervising the planting and harvesting.

Nights were quite a different matter. He could not lose the feeling of having failed abjectly in his military career. Sleeplessly he would relive every step of the trail that had led to the bloodshed at Monongahela. How culpable had he himself been? He knew the Indian mind. He knew the tactics of the French.

He should have done more.

Granted he was a junior officer. Granted that Braddock had been a crusty, difficult general. Granted even that he had tried to give the old commander his views.

There was the rub.

Should he not have been more insistent? Being a volunteer officer had been difficult but he had been sought out for the very reason that he knew the terrain. Should he not have spoken individually to the other officers, tried to wheedle or pound some sense into the heads of Shirley and Burton and St. Clair, then let them go to the general?

It might have worked.

"I gave up too easily," he told himself as he stood at the window and watched the sun rise over the eastern fields. "Technically, maybe even before God, morally, I was not wrong, but I could have done more."

The praise that was being heaped on him for his bravery in battle only served to sting him. He was not so dishonest that he would not admit to himself that he had proven a good officer under fire. But little comfort that would be to the families of those soldiers who had been massacred.

His remonstrations always ended on a grim note. If there could be a lesson learned from the whole of the disgrace, it was this: Never again would he hold his tongue when he knew he was in the right. Henceforth he would speak his mind plainly and forcibly.

There would be another campaign, he was sure of it. But if he were to have a part in the next one, he would go with untied hands.

The call came much sooner than he expected. Governor Dinwiddie barely digested the scope of the disaster before he realized that an even worse disaster had been foreshadowed. The retreating troops had in effect cut a road by which the French could easily march from the Ohio clear down to Virginia. There was absolutely no question but that a new offensive had to be planned at once. Besides, the Indians had become so bold that settlers in Augusta County were being scalped and their homes destroyed. The wanton murders must be terminated.

When the General Assembly met on August 5, 1755, it decided that the remainder of the Virginia Regiment was to be reassembled and sent to the frontier to deal with the savages and the French.

The news interested George greatly but he didn't attend the session. He would not again go on an expedition where whatever skill and knowledge he possessed would not be used because of his lack of authority. His feelings were known. Letters came from Williamsburg, cautiously asking what terms he would wish if he were chosen to command the regiment. Then word was discreetly sent that the governor was indeed interested in making him commander of the forces and that it would be a good idea if he came to the capital for a discussion.

The faint weakness still persisted but George could not deny that he looked forward to the interview. The crotchety old governor irritated him immensely but he could not help but feel sorry for him. Dinwiddie wanted to get back to England. He wanted to go to Bath and look after his health, but understandably he did not want to lay aside his responsibilities until the sorry chapter of disgrace of the Colonial forces had been rewritten.

As a man and an officer George understood and sympathized, even while he ruefully admitted that with all this, Dinwiddie would undoubtedly create obstacles to the proper conduct of any campaign.

The trouble began before he even got to Williamsburg. He'd written that he would only accept command if he had a voice in selecting the officers who would be on his staff. Characteristically Dinwiddie went ahead and appointed captains for almost all the companies that would form the Virginia Regiment.

The scene with the governor was a stormy one. The ailing old man demanded to know why Colonel Washington would not accept the honor of the position he was being offered.

George stood at attention while the tirade went on. He was angry clean through and his many lessons in childhood of not showing emotion during his mother's rantings served him well.

He was human enough to be pleased that indirectly the governor was paying him a compliment. The men had little taste for this new campaign, especially after hearing about the scalpings and torture that had taken place after Monongahela. What the governor was actually saying was that Colonel Washington was held in such high esteem for his bravery, and was so loved by his men, that morale would be increased a thousand-fold if he were to head the regiment. The governor concluded on a somewhat irrational note. "And since your country so honors you, it is your duty to accept your country's wishes."

"Because I have given my best, I must give more . . ." The inconsistency stirred a moment of amusement in George, but it was short-lived. The insinuation that he was not ready to do further duty stung him. "I assure Your Excellency that it is in part my desire not to lose the esteem that my country has been pleased to bestow on me that makes me adamant now."

He was not let off with that. The legislators of the House of Burgesses were called in to trample on the arguments George offered. They raised his pay; they granted an allowance for his table. "The officers," he repeated, staring at Dinwiddie, "the officers."

At last compromise was reached. George was permitted to name his field officers. When that offer was made, he stopped arguing. Compromise, yes, but a workable one. He could go ahead with confidence. His yes was accepted with alacrity, although he heard Dinwiddie mutter something about upstart young officers, meaning himself, he supposed.

He found that he needed whatever confidence he could muster in the next few months. As soon as he was back in service the old problems returned tenfold. Supplies were hard to obtain. It was one thing for the legislature to vote taxes to pay the expenses of the regiment, quite another thing to collect them. The men were terrified at the tales of the Indians and sharp discipline had to be put into effect to toughen their backbones.

Still, all his orders lacked teeth without clear-cut military law to deal with deserters and insubordinate officers. He struggled with the problem from August till October. Then he settled his troops at Fort Cumberland and returned to Williamsburg for the session of the General Assembly. There he discovered that the governor had at last recommended that military law be tightened to deal with deserters and draftees who failed to report.

He stayed a few days at Williamsburg with friends. By now the report of the activities at Monongahela had been enriched with the passing of time. They had not fought three hundred Indians but sixteen hundred. All the British Regulars had fled, or so went the story. General Braddock had been wounded then rescued from the savages by the Virginia troops under Colonel Washington's command. The British Regulars had left him to be scalped.

George was honest enough to be distressed, human enough to enjoy the adulation. As some of his aides commented dryly, they would surely have to pay the balance of the exaggerated praise in the next campaign.

But at the few balls he stayed to attend, George could feel that people were constantly watching him. He had moments of total gratitude to Sally when the ladies complimented him on his graceful dancing. She had taught him well. Always he returned to thoughts of her but he realized that he was looking with rather a new eye at the unattached young ladies. He had a game he played. If one girl seemed more interesting than the rest, he tried to picture her at Mount Vernon. But somehow, no one looked quite right there.

He met many new people those days. One of the couples was Daniel and Martha Custis. Mr. Custis came up to him at one of the balls. "I want to congratulate you on your assignment, Colonel," he said. "We are confident you will speedily attend to our border problems."

George liked the pleasant, firm-speaking man. Daniel Custis was in his mid-forties and looked it even though his hair and mustache were still dark. George had heard that the Custis town house in Williamsburg was famed for its hospitality and that the mansion on their plantation was a showplace. He knew too that Daniel Custis was reputed to be an excellent though scrupulously honest businessman and planter. He realized that Daniel Custis was not expressing perfunctory interest but genuinely wanted to discuss the border problem.

"I don't know how soon we'll settle everything," he said. "The French are entrenched. Our policy toward the natives has been poor. There is much hostility."

Daniel said, "Colonel, let's you and I sit down for a moment. As it is, so much fact and fancy get mixed that I find it hard to believe anything I've heard."

"Certainly," George said, but then a small hand touched Daniel's arm. Both men had been too engrossed to notice that Mrs. Custis had come up and was standing by them. A sheepish look came over Daniel's face. He put his arm around his wife and gently pulled her forward. "All right, my dear, I know I promised not to talk about the border, the French, the governor. What else was I to avoid tonight?"

"That does it, I think." The tone was amused and affectionate and George smiled as Mr. Custis presented him. "Patsy, my dear, I'm sure you know who young Colonel Washington is. My wife, Martha, Colonel Washington."

"I am honored, madame." George realized that Mrs. Custis reminded him of a doll his sister Betty had once had. She was tiny, barely coming up to his chest; she had the same pink-and-white complexion and large brown eyes the doll had had. Her light brown hair was shiny and gathered into curls at the nape of her neck. A pink satin ball gown set off her gently rounded figure.

When she extended her hand, George felt that he had to be careful not to hold it too tightly; it was so small, it seemed lost in his. She acknowledged the introduction then said, "Colonel Washington, surely you did not get away from the trials of war for a few days so that you could refight them in the drawing room. Daniel, my dear, with all the lovely young ladies here, do you really suppose the colonel wishes to talk politics?"

Daniel looked rueful. "Since I never notice the lovely young ladies myself—with one single exception—I forget that they might be of interest to others."

For an instant George felt shut out. The obvious affection between the two, the adoration which Daniel Custis showed when he looked at his young wife—surely she was younger by twenty years—George felt that he was fated always to see and hear affectionate twosomes, to be always only a witness to happiness.

Then Mrs. Custis looked at him and there was earnest

concern in her face. "I promise not to mention the war, but only say how happy we were, Colonel, that you escaped at Monongahela. Your bravery has become legend."

George had learned to accept that compliment gracefully. Why then did it sound as though he'd never heard it before? It was just the tone of sweet sincerity. He bowed and again was aware of the great difference in height between Mrs. Custis and himself. There were times when his great size could still occasionally cause moments of awkwardness. But not now. The admiration that showed in the pretty face that smiled up at him made him feel that he was at least a King's general.

The music was struck up and George was about to ask Mrs. Custis for the honor when she smilingly turned to her husband. "Now you did promise you'd dance a bit," she reminded him. To George she explained, "We're not really very much the dancers, Daniel and I, but there are a few steps I love to do with him."

George watched them as they went onto the ball-room floor. Daniel was stiff and Mrs. Custis danced properly and gracefully but without the flair and instinct of Sally. Then he shrugged impatiently. He did have the gift of finding women most charming when they were irrevocably tied to another man. Resolutely he walked over to one of the pretty Randolph girls. A few minutes later they were whirling around the dance floor and he stopped worrying about the war and about Sally and people who rejoiced in each other and simply enjoyed the fact that he was a good dancer and had an excellent partner.

To her anxious eye his face seemed strained and tired. Christopher materialized to take his hat and gloves, but when she took his hand, it was cold almost to numbness.

Shaking her head, she rubbed first one, then the other of his hands in hers. A glint of amusement showed in his eyes. He bent down to kiss her forehead. "It might take a long time," he murmured.

They'd had a standing joke about her tiny hands and his enormous ones.

"Perhaps the fire will do a more efficient job," she agreed and asked Christopher to bring the general a glass of wine in the study.

They went upstairs together in silence. But once in the study, he heaved a great sigh of relief as he shut the door behind them. He walked over to the fire and spread his hands, flexing the fingers.

She pushed his chair a little nearer the hearth, then

sat down facing it. With visible relief he sank into the comfortable chair, then smiled at her.

He answered her unasked question. "It went very well, I think. Mr. Adams spoke handsomely and his address was well received. He'll make a fine President."

"He's had a fine example."

"Not everybody would agree with that," he reminded her. "Oh, Patsy, I'm glad to be finished. I'm a tired old man."

"I've been calling you an old man for a long time," she reminded him gently.

"But now it's true."

A discreet tap was heard, then Christopher came in bearing two glasses of clear claret.

As Patsy sipped hers she thought how similar this moment was to the afternoon that had begun it all, back at the Chamberlayns' house. After Daniel had died and she'd seen young Colonel Washington again.

"What are you thinking, Patsy?" he asked.

"See if you can guess," she suggested.

"That you're glad it's over . . that you're anxious to go home . . ."

"I'm not looking ahead right now, I'm looking back. Do you remember the first time we sat by a fire together?"

"At the Chamberlayns', you mean." He looked reflective. "What could you have seen in me? I must have looked the scarecrow to you."

"You'd been so ill." She realized that in a way the gaunt fatigue on his face now was what had pulled her mind back to that long-ago afternoon. He'd had the same weariness, the same pallor then.

For a moment they were silent, each absorbed in the memory. Then she felt quick tears in her eyes. She knew he understood them.

"That was the first time I met Patsy and Jacky," he said. "That's what you're thinking."

She barely nodded. "I was thinking about them," she said softly, "and that from that first afternoon, they loved you . . . just as I did . . . just as I did."

WHEN GEORGE RODE UP THE FRONT steps of the Chamberlayns' sprawling manor house, Bishop helped him dismount and took the reins to lead his horse away. Both Bishop and the horse had been the deathbed legacy of Braddock. He'd had them nearly three years now and found it hard to realize he'd ever managed without Bishop. Certainly the man's careful nursing had pulled him through this long siege.

George was dismayed to feel the weakness that still came as soon as he stood on his legs. Well, at least, by heaven, there was something to show for it this time. Not progress, really, but not the amateur performance of being trapped.

Progress. He almost laughed at the word. A year and a half of trying to defend the border with not enough soldiers, not enough supplies, with recruits forever deserting. With the newspapers printing articles on the drunkenness of the officers, as though they'd been having a debauchery in the miserable quarters they'd been forced to use. With the contentious old governor and his own problem about who was in command. For the past year his authority had been challenged by a captain in the British Regulars.

And the illness which sapped his strength so that he could hardly stand. The weeks of doctoring without result. In God's name, he was disgusted. He regretted the impulse that had brought him to this house. He should have ridden on and gone directly to Williamsburg. Sick or well he had to get back to his post. Certainly in his present frame of mind he wasn't fit company for anyone.

He said abruptly, "You'd better eat your dinner early. We'll not stay long."

Bishop was obviously neither offended nor subdued by the brusque tone. "Colonel, sir, you'll feel better once you been inside a bit. You cold and tired now. You have a nice time."

It was for him a fairly personal speech. His concern was more likely to be expressed in his actions and attitude. George smiled wanly, warmed by the man's solicitude, then turned and went up the stairs.

He had expected that there would be other guests.

The Chamberlayns were a large family and their home was always overflowing. They met him in the foyer. Major Chamberlayn pumped his hand, while the major's wife kissed his cheek and commented in shocked tones on his gaunt appearance.

Then they escorted him into the parlor. There were a number of people in the room, but he was not prepared for the person who was sitting quietly in a slipper chair by the roaring fire.

Patsy Custis was dressed in a black gown, which startlingly set off the creamy whiteness of her flawless skin. The soft brown hair that had been bunched in curls at the nape of her neck when he last saw her was now drawn simply into a bun. Little wisps still curled around her forehead, giving her an appealing, childish look. Her brown eyes, large and wide apart in her oval face, had an expression of sadness quite different from the affectionate warmth they'd shown last year.

George hurried through his greetings to the other guests then went over to Patsy. He felt the eyes of the others on him but didn't realize that Mrs. Chamberlayn was deliberately steering them away from the hearth. He was only aware of the quiet figure whose sad face was brightened by her welcoming smile.

"Mrs. Custis—"

"Colonel Washington—" Then her expression became shocked. "Oh, but you haven't been well."

She, of all people, to be so concerned. He brushed aside her reference to his illness. It was he who must properly express sympathy.

"Oh, I'll be quite all right soon. But may I extend my sympathy on the loss of your dear husband."

For an instant there was a suspicion of tears in the large brown eyes but then as she quietly said, "thank you," Mrs. Chamberlayn stepped up to them.

"Yes," she said briskly, "Patsy has had a very bad time and so have you, young Colonel, and now we shall all rejoice that the year is still relatively new and I'm convinced it will be a happy one for all."

Some of the others in the room had heard. There was a ripple of amusement as Major Chamberlayn said, "You must realize, Colonel, that my wife is a perpetual optimist. To her the year is still new in March. She can see spring in the air when in actuality there are ten inches of snow on the ground. And she even insists that all the novels she reads have a happy ending."

Mrs. Chamberlayn was not even slightly discouraged. "Of course I do. Now you must admit you told me that George would never come, and here he is, if somewhat the worse for wear."

George ruefully accepted the judgment of his appearance. He knew his uniform hung loosely on his shoulders, that his color was ashen, his expression drawn. For an instant he had a recollection of the time eight years before when he'd been so sick with the pox and was glad Sally wasn't there to see the harsh pustules.

Why was it that now, he, who was so vain of his appearance—in private meditations with the Almighty he admitted to that sin—was not ashamed to be seen looking like a gaunt scarecrow by Patsy Custis.

Patsy Custis . . . the name brought a question. When the others stopped paying attention, he drew a chair beside hers and said, "Mrs. Custis . . . my curiosity is consuming me. Twice now—at the ball last year and just now—I heard you called 'Patsy.'"

There was a hint of a blush. "My father said that Martha was much too formal a name. He called me 'Patsy' instead."

"It suits you well." George remembered that the first time he'd met her, he'd thought of an exquisite doll. He remembered too the look of absolute love that Daniel had bestowed on his wife. It would not be hard to . . .

With a start he realized that the conversation had once more become general and that Major Chamberlayn was asking him about the last year at the Ohio front.

He leaned forward, slowly turned the glass in his hand, and concentrated on his answer.

"I think that we could have won this war long since except for the fact that we live too long with every problem before it is solved. I can't tell you how impossible it was to maintain discipline before we finally got a deserters' law with some teeth in it. I can't tell you the difficulties with our suppliers. By heaven, we should deal harshly with those men who fatten their pocketbooks on government money and then deliver meat so foul-smelling it has to be buried."

He leaned forward, warming to his subject. "And command. Surely, sir, you know that at the front, in a battle, in a war, on a plantation, in a government, there has got to be a definitive chain of command. Impossible to have the situations such as we've encountered, where a captain with a royal commission plays the king to a captain with a Colonial commission even though the governor has designated the latter as commander."

He finished abruptly, feeling slightly uncomfortable. He was usually too reserved to discuss his opinions or army affairs like this, but the wine, the comfortable room, the balm of being with good friends had loosened his tongue.

He needn't have worried. Major Chamberlayn nodded vigorously. "Of course the trouble originates in

England where our King changes with the opinion of whichever counselor has his ear and will not accept as worthwhile any reports he gets from a Colonial."

"Oh, I don't think it's quite that bad." George was shocked. One simply did not criticize the King.

"I'm speaking the truth," Major Chamberlayn said. "Mark my words, the clash between Colonial and royal commission is only one of a thousand tiny rubs. And it's only the beginning."

"And before you warm to your subject, we shall call a truce." Mrs. Chamberlayn rose gracefully. "I see that dinner is ready."

George rose too and extended an arm to Patsy. With a smile she accepted it and they went into the dining room together.

The long table was filled with all kinds of tempting food but George barely touched it. Anything too rich would still send his system into spasms, and prudently he nibbled on dry bread and sipped clear broth. He could see the concern in Patsy's eyes as she glanced at him from under long lashes. He was seated at Mrs. Chamberlayn's right and Patsy was next to him.

Mrs. Chamberlayn did not comment on his abstinence except to sigh, "Colonel, we shall never fatten you up but perhaps you're wise to be cautious."

The man on Patsy's right was one of the Randolphs,

and George was surprised to hear him ask Patsy how her legal suit was going. It seemed to George a highly personal question to ask and he wondered if she'd show resentment. On the contrary, she seemed almost grateful to answer.

"It drags on so dreadfully." She turned to him. "Colonel Washington, all Virginia knows—but you may not because of your absence—that my husband died without a will. There is the question of a will his grandfather made out and my claim and the claims of my children to the estate are being questioned."

"But of course, you'll win out." Major Chamberlayn's statement was definite.

Patsy nodded. "Yes, I think so, but it is bewildering. Daniel took care of all finances. I never touched them. Now to find myself not only forced to decide on every single expense, but also saying yes and no to lawyers who want to do this and that . . ." She laughed but it was a poor attempt to cover suddenly quivering lips. But then she recovered herself and said briskly, "Never mind. It will be all right, I'm sure."

George thought of his own mother, how she had dissipated her holdings because she too was confused and bewildered by trying to manage her affairs herself. Granted his mother was quite different from the Widow

Custis. The gods themselves would have gotten nowhere in an attempt to help direct his mother in her judgments. Still, a young and pretty woman like Patsy Custis would undoubtedly marry quickly . . . The thought brought chagrin.

It was obviously the same one that Major Chamberlayn had. "Never mind, my dear," he said. "With the suitors already tripping over each other in your parlor, you won't have such problems for too long."

"Now, really." Mrs. Chamberlayn's voice was admonishing.

Patsy smiled. "That I assure you is quite as big a problem as the business arrangements. When Daniel asked me to marry him, I had no question but that he loved me dearly. In fact his father was quite explicit about the fact that I was not Daniel's equal either socially or financially. So when he risked his inheritance by quite simply telling that difficult old man that he loved me well and would marry me, I knew that indeed I was wanted for myself.

"Now when I sit in my parlor with a caller, I wonder if he sees me or the Custis holdings. It's rather hard to decide."

"You will let your heart decide," Mrs. Chamberlayn said.

George laughed, then quickly apologized. "My dear Mrs. Custis, I could only think of my sister Betty, Mrs. Fielding Lewis. When Fielding asked her to marry him, she was not quite sure. He's somewhat older, you realize, and I think Betty was saving her charms for a crown prince at least. When Fielding was having little luck in persuading her, he remembered her childhood dream of a grand house and lyrically described the home he'd build for her. My sister Betty instantly promised to be his bride."

They all laughed. "And it's been a fine match," Major Chamberlayn said.

"An excellent one," George replied promptly. "That's why Fielding himself tells this story with much zest. Betty adores him. He pampers her and, at the same time, almost miraculously remains very much the master of his home."

"You sound as though you approve of a man being master of his home, Colonel," Mrs. Chamberlayn commented a bit dryly. Too late George remembered that in this house the lady had a great deal to say, but he would not be sidetracked.

"I do, madame," he replied. "I think the very word 'husband' bespeaks one who protects and cares for his wife. And surely no woman can be allowed to lead a man around, tweaking his nose—we see it all too often, do we not—and then turn to that same man for the security that is her rightful claim."

He could not help thinking of his own mother. Secretly he'd always suspected that his father was afraid of her. When *he* married—he paused, realizing that he'd used that word in his thoughts many times in the last few hours.

He refused the last course and made a pretense of sipping his wine. Suddenly he was beginning to feel extremely tired again. The aching was returning and the thought of the long journey to Williamsburg wearied him. He decided to rest by the fire in the study for a little while after dinner, then start. With the return of the weakness, a sense of melancholy was beginning to come over him.

Apparently his silence was noticed. The others finished eating quickly, then while some of the guests made ready to depart, Mrs. Chamberlayn escorted him to the study. She tried to persuade him to spend the night.

"Oh, thank you, but I'll have to get on. I'm anxious to see the doctor as soon as possible and get back to my men." He attempted a smile. "It's just that from time to time I find it difficult to believe those who assure me that I'm nearly recovered."

He wondered where Patsy was. He had thought she was staying over but perhaps he had misunderstood. Maybe she had left, too. Or maybe she'd simply gone to her room. Why should she, after all, want to sit with a scarecrow? He was icy cold now and could feel perspiration on his body. Would he never get over these damnable attacks?

Major Chamberlayn came in, stared at him, and said abruptly: "You are spending the night and without argument, sir. I never permit a guest to leave my home after sundown and, besides, you are far from well."

Patsy came in, followed by a servant who was carrying a tray. "I've already sent word to the colonel's servant," she said quietly. "The poor man was standing outside with the horses saddled, stamping his feet with the cold. Colonel, you do inspire loyalty, don't you? From my late husband's estate are 286 slaves and not a one of them would be caught in this blizzard on the chance that I might wish to leave early."

George realized that one of his eyebrows had gone up. His reactions to what was happening were mixed. "You dismissed my man, madame?"

"I told him you were spending the night. You see, you really won't feel much like traveling after you've had this. It will make you quite pleasantly tired."

The servant had put the tray on a table and drawn it up beside George's chair. The tray contained a bowl with a steaming hot mixture.

"What's this?" he asked. Secretly he was dismayed. There wasn't one of his friends who had not subjected him to a homemade remedy in the past months. Invariably he felt worse after all of them.

Patsy pushed the table a bit nearer his chair and handed him the spoon. "Try a little, please."

One sip, he told himself, and no more. With the damnable way his stomach had been acting he'd not risk putting anything into it that might . . . The liquid was hot but not to the point of discomfort. It had a flavor he couldn't quite identify. Meat stock? Some kind of tea?

Patsy did not answer his questioning look. "It's a recipe that has been in my family for generations. And it's quite miraculous when one is getting over a debilitating weakness like dysentery. Now please drink it all. I guarantee you'll feel much better."

He had a feeling the "please" was superfluous. He had a fleeting thought that in the softest possible way Mrs. Custis could probably be quite as adamant as his mother. Oddly the comparison brought amusement. Meekly he drank the contents of the bowl.

Patsy nodded in satisfaction then turned to Mrs. Chamberlayn. "Might we have the fire built up a little? We mustn't let the colonel get a fresh chill."

Mrs. Chamberlayn spoke to a servant at once then turned to her husband. "My dear, we shall leave our young guests for a time. I'm sure they'll excuse us. We'll join them again for a late supper."

Major Chamberlayn looked astonished. "I don't intend—"

His wife slipped an arm through his. "You shall see our guests later."

The harsh aching began to pass and George leaned back in the chair contentedly. Patsy sat opposite him. There was a piece of needlework in a little basket and she picked it up. "I do want you to rest, so please close your eyes, if you wish."

He obeyed again but then found himself unable to keep from looking at her. Through half-closed eyes he watched as the firelight caught the touches of gold in her shiny brown hair. The high-necked, long-sleeved black gown, relieved only by a simple brooch, could not completely conceal the whiteness of her neck and hands. The past year had brought a new maturity to her expression, and, oddly, had at the same time made her seem younger. He tried to imagine her entertaining suitors in her parlor but the picture didn't ring true.

His sister Betty—or Sally—they'd have a wonderful time being courted by half the men in the county. But he suspected that Mrs. Custis would have little taste for flirtations.

The pleasing lassitude brought on by the fire and the broth was playing tricks with George's mind. He felt absolutely at home here, looking across the hearth at Mrs. Custis. A woman like that should never be alone.

Alone. But she had children.

The realization drove sleep away. "Mrs. Custis," he said. "I'm sorry to realize that I haven't inquired about your children. Are they well?"

Patsy smiled. "Quite well, thank you. You'll see them later. They're upstairs in the nursery but their nurse will bring them down to say good-night."

Then she let the tapestry slip unheeded into her lap. "I really wasn't going to bring them this time but at the last minute realized I couldn't leave them. Whenever I have to be parted from them, I'm quite frantic with worry. Of course, they are watched every instant and their nurse is devoted, but I can just see Jacky getting on a horse and galloping by himself—he's four now and very active— and then being thrown. And little Patsy is not quite two but she is so delicate. You see, my first two children died very young and perhaps that's why I'm unreasonably cautious about the two I still have."

"I suspect that every mother worries when her offspring are quite young." George thought that Mrs. Custis had the same look of heartache when she spoke of her children as Anne had had when she discussed the baby. But Anne had been right to fear. She'd lost the baby.

Patsy reached for the tapestry. "I only fear that I shall get worse as they get older. The only word in my own defense is that I truly try to overcome this apprehension."

"Tell me about them." It was not simply a polite inquiry. George realized that he really wanted to hear about the Custis children.

He soon saw that he could not have found a better way to know Patsy Custis. Her expression changed from joy to pride to anxiety to joy again as she discussed her children. "Jacky—a handsome boy, quite willful but so charming that it's difficult to punish him. Daniel found him a handful, I think, and yet was so proud of him. He is so bright. He already has simple lessons which he doesn't like. Little Patsy is so gentle, so anxious to please and be loved. She misses her father, even though she can surely remember him little. When a male visitor comes she studies him for a time, then if he passes inspection, goes and sits uninvited on his lap."

A willful little boy who needed a father's strong hand. A wistful baby girl who needed a father's tenderness. A pretty, young mother.

Almost impatiently George sat up straight, unconsciously tugging at his uniform.

Mrs. Custis smiled. "You're feeling better, aren't you? But at least pull your chair a bit nearer the fire. Otherwise the chill might return."

Now at that point his mother would have harangued about what warfare did to a man's constitution.

And Sally, what would she have done?

He almost laughed. Sally might just have said, "Young Washington, you're feeling fine now. Shall we try the new dance step that Sarah says is the rage in New York?"

As he obediently moved the chair a few inches nearer the hearth, he tried to analyze his feelings. He did not experience a wild pulsing of his senses as he often did in Sally's presence. He did have a feeling that a portion of his heart that had never been touched before was suddenly flooded with warmth.

Mrs. Custis finished an intricate piece of sewing. "Now," she said, "you have listened so patiently to me and, really, it is time for you to tell me about yourself."

"Where shall I begin?"

"At home, I think. Mrs. Chamberlayn tells me you have the most beautiful piece of land in Virginia. Tell me about Mount Vernon."

If she had asked him to speak of himself in any other way, he'd have offered little.

But to speak of Mount Vernon—to watch the firelight play on the gentle, pretty face across from him as he described the roll of the land, and the house, being honest enough to protest its present inadequacies. To speak of his plans for house and land, and where flower beds would eventually grow and where shrubbery would line the approaches.

He talked for a long time and realized that other names were creeping into the conversation—his mother, his brothers, the Fairfaxes, the days in Barbados with Lawrence. He talked until the logs split and collapsed into blazing embers, and then, realizing that the room was suddenly chilly, sprang to his feet.

"Mrs. Custis, my apologies. Loquaciousness is not usually one of my vices but you are too polite and too good a listener for your own comfort."

She got up easily. "If there are apologies due, they are mine to give. I've enjoyed this so much and I think that now I hear the children coming to say good-night."

The door of the study burst open, and a whirlwind raced in, a little boy with bright brown eyes and hair falling on his face. He ran up to Patsy. "Mother, it's really too early to go to bed, isn't it?" He started to trip over his own feet and automatically George reached out and caught him.

The wide brown eyes widened even more.

"Oh, sir, I'm sorry. Are you . . . ? In the nursery they said . . . Sir, are you Colonel Washington, the hero?"

George laughed. "I'm Colonel Washington, young man."

Jacky inhaled sharply. "Upstairs they told us not to carry on because you were visiting and you're used to order and having people doing what you say. Is that right?"

"Quite right, and you must be Jacky. And as a good soldier, you would not question an order to retire."

Jacky brushed aside the reference to bedtime. "May I try on your sword?"

George laughed again. He went over to the corner of the den and got it. "You may not take it from its sheath. And you may not swing it. Have I made myself clear?"

"Perfectly, sir." Jacky's mouth was a wide O. "Did you kill many Indians with it, sir?"

"I lost count after twenty."

"Twenty!"

"Jacky, you must not annoy the colonel." Patsy looked perplexed. "And where is little Patsy? Oh . . ." The little girl came into the study, holding her nurse's hand. But she dropped the hand and ran to her mother. Patsy picked her up and said, "This is my baby, Colonel."

George felt disconcerted as he looked into the solemn brown eyes of the little face that was appraising him so intently. Remembering how he'd first greeted Anne's infant, he reached out one finger. Somewhat to his amazement little Patsy took it and smiled.

"You have won her," Patsy said. "In a moment she'd

be wanting to go to you, but I'm sure you want rest more than a romp before supper. Now Jacky, say good-night to Colonel Washington and give him back his sword."

With a long sigh the little boy obeyed but as he relinquished it said, "Colonel Washington, would you like to visit us sometime?"

George said, "I'd like to very much. In fact, I was about to ask your mother if I might call after I leave Williamsburg next week. You will be home then, I think?"

He was looking at Jacky but addressing the question to Patsy. Her smile was as brilliant as her son's as she said, "Yes, Colonel Washington, we shall be home and so happy to receive you."

Jacky said, "We live near Williamsburg, Colonel. Everybody knows where. Just ask people where the White House is. That's the name of our home."

George looked at the little group in front of him. They made a charming cameo against the dying firelight and the deepening shadows. It seemed so absolutely right that they were looking at him, that they were here with him. For a moment his mind seemed to play tricks and he could see these three on the steps of Mount Vernon, watching for him to ride home. He could see little Patsy and Jacky romping on the sloping lawns near the Potomac. He could see Patsy as mistress of his home.

He extended his hand to Jacky, who took it solemnly. "The White House," he said. "No power on earth shall keep me from it."

DINNER WAS ONLY FOR THE HOUSEHOLD; for the wonder of it, no guests had managed to get invited. And yet, Patsy thought, with a touch of amusement, the general's notion of dining alone completely ignored the fact that they never had less than eight or ten at the table.

During dinner she eyed Nelly and young Washington and found comfort in the fact that neither seemed anything but delighted at the prospect of going home. But they had been well trained. It had taken her too long to let George really help with the raising of little Patsy and Jacky. With Jacky's children it had been different. When they'd come to Mount Vernon, "Grandpapa" had been their father. She hadn't made the mistake of standing between them as she'd tried to do when her own children were young.

But that was a long time ago.

Young Lafayette was in high spirits. He loved Mount Vernon, too. He and his affable tutor would be welcome guests there. Again her eyes seemed to play tricks. Young Lafayette was so like his father . . . Nelly was like little Patsy . . . young Washington like Jacky. A generation had gone by since those others sat around a dinner table with George and her. As long as *he* was always with her . . .

He'd suggested that she rest after dinner. A public reception was scheduled for the evening, to honor him. They'd thought that the magnificent birthday honors of only two weeks before would spell the last of the ceremonies. He had been only somewhat pleased at this final good-bye, but she understood why. To her it seemed that his countrymen were letting him go so reluctantly that they seized at opportunities to see him again.

Then Nelly said, "Grandpapa, I thought that was a very fine toast at dinner last night."

Whenever George's eyes rested on Nelly, they lost their habitual look of reserve and became affectionate. With a touch of amusement in his voice he said, "I rather thought you were too interested in the flattery of your dinner companion to hear any stuffy toasts."

Young Washington and Lafayette laughed and Nelly shook her head with a mock frown. "Now Grandpapa . . ."

"I agree, sir," Lafayette said. "I could not help wishing my father might have heard the words." With a ring in his voice he repeated them: "'Ladies and gentlemen, this is the last time I drink your health as a public man. I do it with sincerity and wishing you all possible happiness.' It was very moving, sir."

"The British minister's wife wept," Nelly said.

George pushed back his chair. "Then she weeps easily." His tone was dry. "My dear . . ."

Patsy rose with him. Together they went upstairs but, while she went in to rest, he went directly to his desk in the study. He and Lear would have to begin packing the papers and files immediately. He wanted to be out of this house and on the way. He groaned inwardly at the prospect of organizing his Presidential papers once he got home, to say nothing of the state to which his personal papers had been reduced. Even this important work had to be balanced with repairing the property. Much, much needed doing at Mount Vernon.

But somehow the prospect of all the tasks was exhilarating. Lately, this last year especially, a new problem in government, a new squabble between the Congress or the cabinet, a new situation that was potentially explosive, brought a sense of weariness to him—an almost physical feeling of a burden on the shoulders. He had joked about having a pair of sixes on his shoulders on his last birthday, and the joke really explained the way he felt. He did indeed have the sensation of weights pressing him down.

That feeling was sure to vanish soon. The papers stopped rustling in his hand. He wondered if the fence required whitening and indeed how much painting might be necessary. He would have many visitors; small hope that he'd be left in perfect retreat. He wanted to show off Mount Vernon properly when they came. It should be glistening and perfect—a well-rubbed jewel.

George stood up and with characteristic neatness folded the papers in his hand and put them back in the drawer of the desk. He would take a short rest before the reception. A moment later, as he sat braced on the study chair while Christopher pulled off his boots, he was still making mental notes of minor repairs to Mount Vernon.

Fortunately they'd be arriving in time to attend to any spring transplanting. He was anxious to see how the bowling green would look this spring. He felt that it greatly enhanced the approach to the mansion.

Long ago he'd had all these plans for landscaping. Year by year he'd inaugurated them. Of course, he first tested them on Patsy. She had a discernment that made her able to envision an overall effect from a quick sketch or a description.

The boots were off. George flexed his feet and leaned back, closing his eyes. Poor Patsy. How she'd needed her imagination when as a brash young officer he'd taken her from the tranquil beauty of the White House and brought her to the neglected plantation that was Mount Vernon . . .

S EVERAL WEEKS PASSED FROM THAT DAY at the Chamberlayns' until the afternoon he rode briskly up the tree-lined driveway to the lovely mansion that was the Custis plantation home.

During those days he'd made great progress toward getting over his illness. He was still painfully careful about what he ate, but for the most part the distressing ailment had run its course. He'd regained a few pounds and his coat didn't look as though it were hanging from a skeleton.

He thought that perhaps the reason his spirits were so buoyant during those weeks was that he was in better health. But he also admitted that his meeting with Patsy Custis and his anticipation of seeing her again contributed to his well-being.

A certain nervousness went hand in hand with that anticipation. When he reflected on that afternoon by the fire in the Chamberlayn study, he wondered if he and Mrs. Custis would recapture that quality of rapport and understanding, or had it been one of those rare meetings of spirit that are not easily duplicated?

It was with a feeling of uncertainty at the outcome of his visit that he began the ride from Williamsburg to the plantation on the Rappahannock. Bishop accompanied him and when they reached the Custis property he clucked appreciatively at the well-kept fields. When they dismounted at the steps, a liveried servant was waiting to take the reins. "You must be Colonel Washington." The man's perfect teeth were revealed in a brilliant smile. "They sure is expecting you inside."

As George tossed him the reins, an upstairs window was thrown open and he could hear Jacky shouting, "He's here! He's here!"

He started up the steps quickly. Whatever doubts he had had about this visit vanished.

Patsy was standing at the doorway. She was wearing a simple blue gown that clung softly to her body. Her eyes were sparkling today and the gladness in her whole manner presented as hearty a welcome as her son's loud cry.

As he came to her, she reached both hands out and impulsively he lifted them to his lips. Her first words were a comment on his appearance. "Oh, Colonel Washington, you look quite recovered. I'm so glad."

Then as he walked into the foyer with her, Jacky

came racing down. "I told you he'd come, Mother," he announced triumphantly.

Patsy blushed and George shook Jacky's hand gravely.

"It's just that I didn't want to see them disappointed," Patsy explained. "I knew it was quite possible your plans might change."

So she too had wondered about that afternoon— wondered if he would change his mind about the visit. He addressed himself to Jacky. "Young man, you were quite right to be sure you could anticipate my call today. For one thing, I had to thank your mother for the diet she gave me. Thanks to her I'm quite well again."

The inside of her home was exactly what he'd expected. Clean and restful, smelling faintly of beeswax and fresh greens, stately mahogany polished till it shone with a fine patina. Warmth and comfort, elegance and good taste, an overall sense of harmony. He ruefully thought of the hodgepodge effect of the decor at Mount Vernon.

As a special favor the children were allowed to dine with them. Jacky ate heartily and quickly although his table manners somehow managed to remain excellent. Little Patsy barely nibbled at the small amount of food on her plate and finally her mother took a spoon and began to feed her.

"You will never be strong, dearest, if you don't eat better." The voice was lightly chiding but George realized that the little girl's health always had her mother desperately worried.

After dinner, little Patsy was put in for a nap and George and Patsy strolled through the grounds. Jacky accompanied them. One minute he was in back of them, then between them, then far ahead, then trailing behind.

Patsy introduced George to her overseer. George sincerely congratulated the man on the splendid appearance of the entire plantation and quickly found himself in a discussion on the relative merits of several tobacco plants. He hesitated to comment when asked for an opinion, but the subject was of great interest to him and clearly the Custis overseer was an intelligent farmer. George and he were soon in deep discussion over the advisability of rotation of fields. Jacky began to fidget. Absentmindedly George reached out and put a restraining hand on the boy's arm and was somewhat astonished to see that Jacky immediately quieted down. He did remember to preface his remarks with comments like "Of course, Mrs. Custis shall decide but this is how I would be governed in making a choice."

It was obvious that Mrs. Custis welcomed advice. Again he was struck by the realization that this was not a woman who enjoyed the freedom of making her own decisions.

When he left that day, it was with the understanding

that he would come soon again. The new governor was due, and when His Excellency arrived in Williamsburg, he, George, would be expected to call on him.

It was May before he returned. Williamsburg was in the height of the social season but Patsy assured him that she had been out little, nor had she had many guests. It was obvious to him that she had left her time free to be sure not to miss his visit.

The thought of her willingness to adjust her own plans to his was both pleasant and disturbing. He would be going back to the front, and might be gone a long time. Should he address himself to Patsy? That visit was a troubled one. He sensed his own reserve and knew that it could easily be interpreted as disinterest or moodiness. After a time Patsy's sparkle diminished and his silence found an equal in hers.

Even the children sensed the change in atmosphere. Little Patsy wept easily and Jacky vied for his attention with a running chatter that became irritating.

Their mother tried to placate them but then after a time gave a rueful little laugh. "You see, Colonel Washington," she said, "children are not always charming and obedient. In fact, many days they are quite difficult. But of course a parent understands that."

The sentence hung between them. In effect, she was stating the fact that not every man cared to assume the guardianship of another man's children. In effect, she was saying that she believed that he was not going to offer to share the raising of hers.

That day when he left, he told her that she should begin to enjoy the society of her friends again. He did not mention a return visit.

But three weeks later he was back. His orders had come. The final march on Fort Duquesne was to begin. And lying awake through sleepless nights, George had realized that he could not risk losing Patsy Custis.

It was clear that she was not prepared for his address. Her glad exclamation when he arrived was quickly subdued into an attitude of courtesy without special overtones. Clearly she had decided that the bachelor colonel would remain a bachelor and she did not intend to let her own feelings for him be known.

Jacky was unaware of the subtleties. His unfeigned delight at seeing his hero was as artless as it was noisy. Finally George said firmly, "Young Master Custis, there is quite an important matter I must discuss with your mother. You will go to your nurse and stay with her until you are called."

"But . . ." Jacky got ready to make his protest.

"Now!" His command was uttered in precisely the same tone he would use to a recalcitrant private.

Jacky scurried out of the room and George took

Patsy's hand. He kept their fingers linked together as he said, "I have a feeling that young Master Custis and I may lock horns from time to time but it will be good for him, I think."

Patsy's astonishment at the statement was quite as real as her son's reaction to the order to leave.

For a moment George felt tongue-tied but, as usual, he expressed himself through Mount Vernon.

"I feel very much like the father who is offering a very awkward daughter," he smiled. "And yet, like that father, I hope that another's eyes may see the promise of beauty that exists."

Now he raised her hands so that they touched his lips. "Patsy, in these past weeks I have thought of nothing but you. There will never be joy for me if I go away without knowing that you and your children are waiting for me to come home."

Her blush was as real as any young girl might have shown on being addressed by her first suitor. Amusement at the thought made it easy for George to draw her close to him. She had been married nearly ten years, she had been a mother four times over, yet it was he, the bachelor, who was the least nervous of the two.

Unbidden, the thought of Sally Fairfax came to his mind. When he danced with her, her tall slenderness made even his great height seem balanced.

On the other hand, at this moment as he took Patsy Custis into his arms, her very smallness made him feel overwhelmingly protective.

If Sally challenged him, Patsy gave him faith in himself. With her he would find his challenges on the outside—in attending to his estate, in seeing to a political career in Burgesses, in finishing with this damnable dragged-out war.

His hand smoothed the back of her hair. With his other hand he tilted her chin up. The smile on her lips and in her eyes showed no sign of timidity. It was the expression of a woman who was used to being deeply loved.

For the first time he kissed her on the lips. And again, unwillingly, he compared her with Sally. Even the casual public kisses he'd exchanged with Sally—at moments of farewell or greeting after a long absence—quickened his senses. From the lips of Patsy Custis he found warmth . . . and more. He realized that their kiss might have been the affectionate exchange of a couple long used to each other. It was as though for them there would be no hesitation, no awkwardness in their love, but rather an early contentment that was delightful and welcome.

It was obvious Patsy thought so too. She lifted her hands and cupped his face between her palms. "My old man," she said, smiling, "offering your dearest possession, Mount Vernon, to me and the children to be our home, and then trying to be honest about its shortcomings. You sounded so distressed."

They laughed together. It was the first time she had called him her old man, but somehow he knew it would not be the last.

It was not the first time he had witnessed her discernment. Patsy might be a very feminine woman who wanted a man to make her decisions for her but she had an insight that made him wonder sometimes if she could indeed read his mind.

He had thought of Patsy sharing his home, sitting opposite him at the table, being his hostess. He realized that he knew so little he had never really considered that she would be sharing his hopes and dreams and plans too. The thought was exhilarating.

"Shall we not summon Master Custis?" he laughed. "I am sure he is quite put out with me and it's high time I restore myself to the good graces of my new son."

IS HEALTH AT LAST RESTORED, HE returned to the military post at Winchester. And finally, it seemed, his arguments about carrying the war into the French-held territory were to be heeded—not that he flattered himself by thinking the military strategy was being changed because of his advice. But the brutal attacks of the savages on the settlers, the endless raids and harassments did make it clear that the enemy must be destroyed at the source. Going to Williamsburg to explain the military situation to the Congress had been helpful. George could see that many members were at last impressed by his constantly repeated statement, "The French simply have to be driven from the Ohio."

Two changes made it easier. General Forbes was put in command and Governor Fauquier was appointed. On these new leaders George constantly impressed the need for speed. Speed was essential. The friendly Indians were becoming impatient, and these allies must not be lost.

He was sent with his regiment to Fort Cumberland. And, at last, concrete plans were formed for a siege at Fort Duquesne.

Once that fort was retaken he would leave the army. His goal would be achieved.

And there was much to be done. These evenings were not quite so hard to endure because suddenly a life at Mount Vernon had become a reality again. Soon he would be finished with the army. Soon he would be marrying Patsy Custis. Soon he would be standing for a seat in the House of Burgesses.

He spent every spare hour planning alterations and repairs to Mount Vernon and sending detailed letters to the contractor who was handling them. George William Fairfax kept an eye on the progress and reported to him.

He had tried to write to Sally about his engagement. A dozen times he started a letter, a dozen times he tore it up. And then in the end she heard about it from someone else, probably someone from Williamsburg in whom Patsy had confided.

Her letter was light and joked about the pretty widow whom he was courting. But for all its airiness there was a strain of sadness there, too.

Sally would be genuinely happy to see him with a wife installed in Mount Vernon. Sally loved her husband.

But he knew that it wasn't just vanity on his part to believe that she cared about him, too. It wasn't just a one-sided attraction.

Suppose, after all, they had met while she was still free, before she married George William.

At that thought George reluctantly smiled. When Sally married George William, she had been eighteen. At that time he himself had been only sixteen. Small chance he would have had of having his courtship accepted then.

But now it was ten years later. The age difference between himself and Sally meant nothing. It was totally unimportant. If they were meeting now for the first time . . . if they were free . . . what would it be like? Then he faced the question that had been nagging at his subconscious. If Sally were ever free would he regret that he was not? In the torment of his soul he wrote to her: "Do not tease me about the pretty widow when you know whom it is I truly love."

Her answer treated his letter lightheartedly. Once again he wrote, "Can you possibly misunderstand?"

While he waited for her reply, George felt that he was living in a vacuum. Mechanically he gave orders, saw to the preparations for the march on Duquesne. He was a good soldier, a good commander. He could trust a subconscious part of his mind to take over the decision-making area and do it well. He felt himself to be a spectator on a high hill observing the group in the valley below. He felt himself an observer of himself.

And, as usual, it was Mount Vernon that saved him. His letters to Patsy were cold, almost businesslike. He signed them, "Your affectionate friend." Afterward, waiting for a reply, he miserably expected reproaches.

But when Patsy's letter came, it was filled with inquiries about Mount Vernon. Would he please draw her a sketch of the layout of the house? She would be bringing some furnishings from the White House. But, of course, she wanted to please him. She wanted her belongings to blend properly with his. Tell her about the china and linens . . . and the pictures. Which of the furniture at the White House did he feel would be a complement to Mount Vernon's possessions?

A sigh escaped George as he read the letter. Like a cool refreshing breeze blowing away the cloying heat of the day, the letter erased the frantic restlessness, the oppressive emotions of the past weeks. George sat down at the desk, smoothed the note out in front of him, and reached for pen and paper. He frowned in concentration as he tried to remember exactly the inventory of his present furnishings and what new pieces he had ordered from his agent.

In his meditation he forgot that the mail had brought

no letter from Sally. He even forgot that he had been so anxiously awaiting one. His mood was no longer of torment or anxiety but anticipation and planning. He dipped his pen into the ink and quickly began to write:

"My Dearest Patsy . . ."

NEARLY THREE HUNDRED GUESTS WERE present at the farewell dinner. It was held at Rickett's Amphitheater and preparations were elaborate. The majority of the assemblage gathered at the Oeller's Hotel next door then marched into the amphitheater to the tune of "Washington's March."

George could feel Patsy's quiet pride in this final ceremony honoring him. For his part he could only want to get it over. His mind was racing ahead—the serious packing could at last begin in the morning. How many days would it take to finish the task? Three, four, not more than that surely.

Nelly was lovely, her hair piled on her head, her shoulders and neck creamy above her low-cut formal gown. Already so many young men hovered around her but she disdained them all. Well, give her time. He was in no rush to lose her. He and Patsy liked having the young people around.

He had heard rumors of a surprise that would be

exhibited that night, but he wasn't prepared for the magnificent painting of himself that was unveiled. It was a transparency by Charles Peale. George liked Peale's work well, and this portrayed himself in a full-length portrait. It wasn't a bad likeness either and heaven knows he usually didn't care for portraits of himself. He did not consider vanity one of his cardinal sins but he did feel that most of his portraits gave him a stiff unbending expression that he honestly didn't consider typical. Of course the damnable teeth that had plagued him all his life were first in his mind when he was being sketched and maybe that self-conscious look was a tribute to the artist's skill.

Patsy didn't think so. Patsy always sighed that it was a real pity no artist existed who could properly catch the man he was. She was studying the picture and as he glanced at her she squeezed his hand. "My old man," she murmured, so softly that it would have been impossible for another ear except his to catch the phrase.

In the Peale painting the figure "Fame" was holding a laurel wreath over George's head. There were surrounding characters which someone explained symbolized the gratitude of the people.

In the background of the picture Peale had drawn Mount Vernon. George felt a flash of amusement. If the entire piece was a little too sentimental for his taste, he felt real gratitude that Peale had so successfully caught the dreamlike loveliness of Mount Vernon.

Then the moment of humor passed and George realized it had only been a camouflage for deep feeling. How kind this assemblage was, how kind the planning and execution of this tribute. There were many who would rejoice with journalist Bache that his administration was at an end, but there were more, many more who would believe that he had done his best.

He realized that he heartily wished his mother might have been here to share this tribute. God knows there were not many times in his adult life when he'd felt a longing for her presence, but he did know she'd be pleased at this. Long ago he'd told her that he would attempt to live up to her family motto, and the Ball family had chosen a lofty one: "Aspire to the Heavens."

Dinner followed the unveiling. Not dinner, really, but a feast. George looked around the crowded table. So many of the people here would be passing from his life forever. Ambassadors changed, elected officials went home, either by their own volition or by the will of the public—surely no society was as flexible as the one consisting of public officials. Many of these people had been guests at the Executive Mansion scores of times. Some few would undoubtedly find their way down the Potomac to visit him again but for the most part this was a real farewell.

He picked up his knife and fork. Under the touch of melancholy a vibrant exultation began surging like a charge of energy through him. When he and Patsy finished eating, they could decently withdraw. He might even be able to spend an hour or two sorting his papers tonight. If Lear had gotten the crates out, he might even do some actual packing.

It was not much later that he touched Patsy's arm. "My dearest?" Her nod was almost imperceptible. But it answered two questions. No, it was not too early to withdraw. Yes, she was quite ready to leave.

When they stood up to go, the assemblage rose to its feet. The band immediately played and applause and music mingled in the chamber.

Once in the carriage they both leaned back and sighed. "I hear they have a very stirring toast to make for you," Patsy said. She frowned in concentration. "It goes like this: 'May the evening of your life be as happy as its morning and meridian have been gloriously useful.' Jefferson told me that that was the one selected after many were offered. I think it quite lovely and most appropriate."

"The evening of my life will be gloriously useful these next few days," George commented. "Patsy, I really dread the preparations for this move. We seem to have accumulated so much. The carriages will break under the weight of all that we're taking with us to Mount Vernon."

The coachman turned the horses into the driveway of the Executive Mansion. As the carriage swayed, Patsy leaned against him and then lingered an instant against his shoulder. "You used exactly the same words to me on another journey," she reminded him. "Can you remember which one?"

The carriage stopped and Christopher was already waiting to open the door. George paused before descending. "Most certainly, I can," he replied calmly. He got out of the carriage and reached his hands up to assist her. "It was in the spring of '59 when I brought the new Mrs. Washington and her children to Mount Vernon for the first time."

THEY WERE MARRIED ON JANUARY 6, 1759. Somehow he survived—but survive wasn't the word at all, of course. Maybe it described his coping with the incredible number of people, the festivities, the awkward business of being the center of attention at an affair which had no element of familiarity. He'd gladly face another Monongahela ambush instead.

But the ceremony itself was quite different. Patsy again reminded him of Betty's childhood doll as she stood beside him. Even with her hair piled high on her head, she barely approached his shoulder. She wore a yellow brocade dress that parted to reveal a silver-and-white petticoat, violet silk slippers, and pearls. He wore his dress uniform of blue and scarlet. When they exchanged their vows, he was able to forget the assemblage and the fact that he simply could not speak in public; he realized only that her eyes had that wonderful mixture of happiness and gentle concern for him—maternal and childlike—how could a woman mix those ingredients?

Afterward the party went on for hours. The governor

himself attended and half the legislature. George groaned when he realized that the White House was bursting with overnight guests. But finally they were able to slip upstairs. Before they went to their chamber, they stopped to look at the sleeping children. Patsy kissed both foreheads and he almost followed her example but decided against it. God forbid Jacky should wake up at that point.

Then the door of the bedroom closed and they were alone. Alone. He felt that some move, some gesture was surely expected of him. He felt quite simply frozen and for the first time since he was sixteen hopelessly aware of his great height.

And, of course, Patsy understood. She came over to him and said casually, "I told my maids not to wait up for me. Will you . . . ? Fumbling and awkward, he unhooked the clasps that held her necklace.

Then she turned to him and her smile was gentle and loving. "Was it such a terrible ordeal for you?" A decanter was on the table by the fireplace. She poured the pale sherry into two glasses and handed one to him. Settling in one of the fireside chairs, she slipped off her pumps. "My poor old man." At her affectionate tone he tentatively sat in the seat opposite.

"I'm so flattered that the governor attended," Patsy said. "It can only prove his fine opinion of you. He refuses dozens of invitations to lovely parties right in

Williamsburg. And here he has taken this trip just to see you married."

"There is the chance that he came to honor the lovely bride." George gratefully realized that he had recovered his voice.

Patsy shook her head. "I think the bride fitted rather nicely into the long shadow cast by the groom." She slipped from her chair and walked over to his. Taking his right hand with both of hers, she raised it to her face. "The bride is quite content always to live like that."

THEY SPENT THE LATE WINTER AND EARLY spring at the Custis town house in Williamsburg where George, as a new member of the House of Burgesses, attended the legislative sessions.

Williamsburg was very gay that season, a gaiety that reflected the joy in the recapture of Fort Duquesne. For George that social season was a revelation. He enjoyed attending the balls with Patsy on his arm and he soon learned that he'd never really known what was going on at a party before. Long after they returned home from the various social events, they would lie awake, her head on his shoulder, while she gossiped to him about who said what, who was being linked with whom, the nuances and undercurrents that seemed to be the prerogative of the female.

He learned that Patsy's information was remarkably accurate. If she heard from the ladies that this one's husband would support a measure in the assembly, or the governor was displeased with an approaching bill, and this long before His Excellency had so much as hinted at his displeasure, she was inevitably right. George found that instead of tolerantly saying, "My dear Patsy, how could your ladies know about such matters," he was looking forward to her latest nuggets.

Once he ruefully laughed, "If I ever find myself in a military situation again, it will be a strong temptation to use a lady as a spy. I'd win the war in a week."

He had been afraid that bachelorhood would be a difficult habit to break. He was used to living alone, not being responsible for or to anyone on a family level. To his delight he found that his and Patsy's personalities meshed so smoothly that it seemed impossible to imagine he had not always shared a life with her.

He knew that often he was quite silent—the habit, he guessed, of long hours at Mount Vernon when he'd had only servants for company. Or, maybe, that reserve was the result of the ranting sound of his mother's voice, which in childhood had made him retreat into himself.

But if Patsy ever found him too quiet, she gave no indication. She would chat on, satisfied with only a nod or an occasional remark. On the other hand, his very calmness was good for her. If she had a weakness, it was her unrelenting worry about the children. If little Patsy refused to eat, her mother could be reduced almost to tears. Jacky was a lively, active child, who would not walk when he could run, and who seemed to delight in terrifying his mother by performing daredevil stunts in her presence.

Patsy was delighted to turn over her financial matters to the care of her new husband. She told him that she really felt herself to be quite thrifty in household management, although sometimes she was perhaps too extravagant when ordering her wardrobe, but he had only to tell her if he was not pleased—this from a woman whose present holdings far exceeded his own.

But on the subject of her children, Patsy simply could not allow either suggestion or help. His tentative remark that perhaps if little Patsy were not made so much of at meals her appetite might improve triggered one of his wife's rare bursts of temper.

"It is easy to make suggestions when you have not watched a baby slip into fainting spells, not seen her fail to gain weight when her playmates are twice her size, not buried her brother and sister." The irritation ended on a sob and a quivering lip. George resolved to bite off his tongue before he interfered again with Patsy's concern over her little daughter.

But Jacky was quite another matter. George could see no earthly reason why a lad of nearly six should be permitted to terrify his mother by the pell-mell manner he raced down the stairs or to slip away from the personal servant, Julius, who had charge of him, and hide while the whole household searched the neighborhood for him and his mother was reduced to near collapse.

He returned from the legislature one afternoon to find that the case. Julius was close to tears, explaining and explaining that he just left Master Jacky for a minute, just a minute, because the boy was in bed for his nap, but when he came back, the boy was gone.

It would have been easier if Patsy were weeping or hysterical, but her drawn, pale face and voice that could not rise above a whisper frightened George more than any outburst could have done.

For his part he felt not the slightest concern for Jacky. He simply didn't believe in a kidnapper, nor did he believe that Jacky had left the house and was wandering around Williamsburg. Just the other night the boy had been talking about the hiding places in this house and how he believed that he could hide for a great long time and never be found.

George called the servants together. They had been going in a dozen different directions, some peering into the street, others aimlessly walking in the yard. He was told that several were searching through the town.

"I believe that Master Custis is playing a trick on us," he said. "I believe he is hiding in this house, perhaps even in his room. Kindly search every closet, under every bed, behind every object of furniture until he is found."

The servants looked incredulous. A faint touch of hope came over Patsy's face, then she rejected the thought and shook her head. While the servants scattered, she said, "Jacky would never do such a thing to me—frighten me for a joke."

George unhooked his sword belt with a slow deliberate movement. He was fighting for time. This was important. If Patsy could only be made to realize that Jacky's inventive scrapes were only a reaching out to find the boundary where he must stop, must behave, she might let him help with the raising of her willful son.

He thought of his mother and the strap she had kept tied to her belt. From earliest memory he had resented both his mother and her free hand with that strap, but in his own way Jacky was clearly showing that he resented unlimited freedom.

He tried to imagine a camp where every private followed his own whims without fear of punishment from the commander. Chaos—the kind of chaos that young Master Custis delighted in causing.

A shout came from upstairs. "Oh, Master Jacky—"

Patsy sprang up, her face flushed, then pale. "Is he . . . he may be hurt—"

But a moment later Julius was coming down the stairs, holding Jacky by the arm. The servant's face held a combination of relief and irritation. "Colonel Washington, sir, he just hiding . . . just like you said . . . just hiding . . . in the closet . . . and all this time . . . his poor mamma—"

"Thank you." George's tone dismissed the man and he left the room. Jacky's triumphant expression changed from mischievous glee to worry as he stared into George's impassive face. He looked to his mother but now Patsy was crying deep, silent tears that pushed each other aside as they hurried down her face. Jacky started for his mother but George caught his arm and swung the boy around to face him.

"Where were you?" The tone of his voice would have made a subordinate officer blanch.

"Oh, sir, I didn't know you were home yet. I thought you wouldn't be home for a bit." Jacky seemed to realize that this time he might indeed not charm his way out of his situation.

"I asked where you were."

"Oh, it was just a game, Poppa." Jacky attempted an ingratiating smile. "I was just hiding. It was fun, everybody calling me . . ."

"And your mother's anxiety. Is that fun?"

Jacky glanced sideways at his mother then quickly looked back. "Oh, Mamma really doesn't mind. She knows I just like to play."

"Does she indeed."

George felt his temper on the verge of going out of

bounds. Deliberately he closed his lips together until he could control himself. When he spoke again, his voice was chipped with ice. "Master Custis, go directly to your room. I shall be right up to you, and I assure you, you will not have any desire to practice pranks for a time."

Jacky turned quickly and raced to his mother, throwing his head in her lap. In an instant George was behind him. He grasped the boy by one shoulder, raised his hand, and gave Jacky a resounding smack across the seat of his pants. "Up to your room, I said."

Wailing, Jacky scurried from the room and George started to follow him. But Patsy pulled at his hand. "You may not punish him—I forbid it—you may not."

George looked down at her, unsmiling. "You seriously believe I will permit Jacky to upset you to this degree and throw this home into such a turmoil?"

"Speak to him, but gently. Explain to him, but don't frighten him. You must not put a finger on him—ever."

"A child cannot grow up without discipline."

"I refuse to let you touch him."

George felt the anger slowly seep from him. "And I wish I had the right to refuse to let you ruin him."

He stalked out of the house. For over an hour he strode through the streets of Williamsburg. Patsy was wrong, wrong, wrong. Yet only the other night she had moaned so piteously in her sleep that he awakened her.

And she had confided the dream that recurred from time to time. In it she walked through a graveyard in which there were only four tombstones. She stopped in front of each one. Two were engraved with the names of the two children she had already lost—the lovely four-year-old Frances and her three-year-old Daniel. But the other two were engraved, too. One said Patsy Custis, the other John Parke Custis. "I will bury all my children," Patsy sobbed as she finished telling the dream. "I know it. I have always known it."

A terrible, terrible fear. Yet little Patsy was indeed a frail child. Could one blame the mother for apprehension?

Of course that fear would ruin Jacky. George blindly followed whatever direction his feet led him. What could he do? At last he started home. When he and Patsy had their own children her apprehension might well lessen. Busy with new babies she would be able to relax her hold on the two children she had. Until then it was pointless to permit Jacky to become a bone of friction. It certainly wasn't the lad's fault that his mother was so shortsighted. George almost smiled. He was very fond of the handsome little boy and, tell the truth, flattered by the way Jacky worshiped him. If he could not use discipline to curb Jacky's mischief and his indolence—it was a struggle to make him do his lessons—he would still guide the child as well as he could.

Finally he turned into the driveway of the Custis house. Obviously he was being watched for, because Bishop was there to open the door. The man bowed without speaking.

Patsy was in the parlor. She had changed her dress to a most becoming pale green afternoon gown that summoned the latent green tone in her eyes. Her eyelids were slightly puffed but other than that there was no sign of her recent outburst. She hurried to him and was waiting to take his hat. "Did you have a nice walk?" Her voice was calm but he could detect her nervousness.

If he were careful, he might still salvage some vestige of authority in his role as stepfather. Patsy was obviously on the defensive. "A walk gives one an opportunity to think . . ." His tone was noncommittal.

"Oh, but I have been thinking, too. You are quite right. Jacky was very naughty. I have sent him to bed without supper." For her it was a great concession.

He smiled almost wearily. "Then at least Master Custis is not totally escaping the consequences of his escapade. That, I suppose, is reassuring."

"No, no . . . and I told him that he must not anger you."

George started to say it was not a case of angering him, then didn't bother. "I shall speak to him myself."

"But you won't—"

"No, my dear, I won't put a finger on him."

He went upstairs to Jacky's room. The boy was in bed although wide awake. He sat bolt upright when George lighted the bedside candle. George nodded to Julius to leave the room, then went over to the bed. "You need not worry. I have not come to give you the punishment you so richly deserve."

Jacky did not look so relieved. "I am sorry I made you angry, Poppa."

"And your mother—"

"Mamma has already said she knows I didn't really mean it—"

"I see." George spotted a tray on the dresser. "I thought you were sent to bed without your supper."

"I was—without a real one. But Mamma said I could have bread and jam and milk in case I got too terribly hungry."

Wordlessly George turned to go. But before he reached the door two arms flung themselves around his legs. He felt Jacky's body shake with sobs as he turned and picked the boy up.

"Now, what's this? You'll have your mother thinking I strapped you inch by inch." One arm held the child close, the other stroked his hair.

"I don't want you to be angry with me, sir. I won't hide again. I promise, I won't. Please don't be angry."

George asked, "Do you want to please me now?"

A vigorous nod.

"Very well." He carried Jacky over to the dresser and together they studied the attractively arranged tray. Crisp bread, a pot of jam, and pitcher of cold milk made George realize that he was starving for his own dinner. "Are you very hungry?" Jackie nodded affirmatively "If you would please me, punish yourself. Don't touch a bite of that food—have absolutely nothing till breakfast. Is that possible?"

Jacky nodded again. George carried the child back to his bed. For an instant he hugged him tightly before he laid him down and covered him. He had Jacky's love, and given even a reasonable amount of control over the lad, he could shape him into a youth to be proud of. Well, time would tell.

He reached over to the table and blew out the candle. "Good-night, my son," he said quietly.

W HEN THE ASSEMBLY SESSION ENDED they left for Mount Vernon. It was on April 2 that the procession pulled out of Williamsburg with crates and trunks and furniture.

George found his emotions mixed. On the one hand he was frantic with desire to see Mount Vernon again, to welcome spring on his own property, to ride over his own fields and see to the planting. On the other hand he was well aware that Mount Vernon was a small house—small compared to the White House, small compared to Belvoir, small compared to his sister Betty's home. Would Patsy be disappointed?

Then he rejected the thought. Of course Patsy wouldn't be disappointed in Mount Vernon. He'd already told her of his plans for adding to the house. But how would Mount Vernon look inside? He had trusted George William to see to the repairs, but no one really had charge of the housekeeping. He'd have to write a note and send it ahead.

They were going to stop at his sister Betty's home overnight. The children were delighted at the prospect of meeting their new relatives and George knew instinctively that Betty and Patsy would like each other well. Betty had long been twitting him about his unmarried state. The strong bond between them had never wavered and whenever he visited Betty at her beautiful home in Fredericksburg, she would good-naturedly lecture him on his need for a wife. He often thought that Betty sensed his devotion to Sally Fairfax because she would make references to finding a nice sensible girl and not wasting his time ending up a crotchety bachelor.

These lectures were always delivered in the presence of her husband. Fielding Lewis and George were great friends. Fielding had won Betty by promising her a beautiful home. He'd kept that promise and their home was one of the showplaces of Virginia. But he'd won her love quite completely on his own merits. They already had two boys and their home was a very happy one. On George's visits, if Betty kept after him too much about his single state, Fielding would say mildly, "My dear, your resemblance to your mother is quite remarkable this evening." Betty would immediately look stricken. "George knows I'm only teasing, now don't you? Very well, not another word."

George thoroughly admired Fielding's deft handling

of his younger sister and was anxious to show his own new family off to him.

And, of course, there was his mother.

Ferry Farm was not far from Betty and Fielding's home and he would take Patsy over to the cold, cheerless house where he had spent his boyhood. He wanted to see his mother, wanted her to see Patsy. It was simply that in her presence his achievements seemed to fall from him. After a comment or two from her he would not be the soldier commander who had helped rescue his colony from terrible danger; he would be the witless fool who had let his plantation run down while he wasted his time running off to war.

Then George's thoughts were pulled back to the present. Little Patsy was crying for a favorite toy which undoubtedly could be found at the bottom of a packing crate. But which one? Utterly impossible to take them all apart. He ordered the procession halted. Patsy and the children were in the carriage. George pulled his horse beside it. She looked up at him, perplexed. Her arm was around the little girl and she was patting her side. "There now, darling," she was saying, "Poppa will get your toy."

Jacky, who had been sulking over not having been allowed to ride his pony next to George, suddenly decided to take a man's stand. "Mamma, don't tell her you'll get her toy. Poppa can't have the crates searched. She will just have to do without it until we get to Mount Vernon in a few days."

The statement made little Patsy's wail become louder. Jacky flashed a man-to-man look at his stepfather. "Young Custis, you have little talent for strategy," George murmured. He realized that it was quite ridiculous to try to solve a family crisis from atop his mount with only his head leaning into the carriage. Swiftly he dismounted and, reaching into the carriage, took little Patsy out. "All right, now, no more tears." He reached for his own immaculate handkerchief and dried her eyes. "Now show me," he commanded, "which crate shall we investigate first?"

Little Patsy looked wide-eyed. "Will you really look for my doll?" Not yet three, she seemed to George a great deal quicker to grasp a situation than her brother. "Most certainly," George promised. "Of course it may take a great part of the day and we won't make Fredericksburg this evening to let you meet your new cousins and see the gift their mother has for you, but of course we shall look for your doll." Little Patsy considered this situation. He was holding the little girl in the crook of his arm. As he waited for her reply he was struck by the almost absolute weightlessness of her body. He fervently hoped that the Potomac country would do her more good than the Rappahannock seemed to have done.

Little Patsy made up her mind. "It'll be all right,

Poppa. We don't have to unpack everything. I'd like to go see my new cousins soon instead."

"Good girl," George said approvingly. He walked over to the carriage and lifted her into it. Patsy looked apprehensive. "We really can't unpack, can we?" Her voice tested the situation.

George smiled at his wife. "No need at all. This very reasonable young lady has decided that her doll is perfectly comfortable and safe in with the luggage and we are going on at once."

He closed the door of the carriage, ignoring Jacky's silent plea to be allowed to ride his pony. Once they got nearer to Fredericksburg he'd let Jacky have his way. But he had no intention of worrying about Jacky set loose on his pony all day.

George made a mental note to be sure to ask Betty to give some small gift to little Patsy. He wryly decided that in the past few months since his marriage he'd had more experience in getting his own way through strategy than ever he'd had at the conference table with Braddock!

It was nearly evening when they arrived at the Lewises' home but there were fires glowing in every hearth. The beautiful house was lighted up in welcome and the pleasure on the faces of Betty, Fielding, and their children was reflected in the radiance on Patsy's face, in the pride with which she introduced her children.

George realized that till now they'd been in Patsy's part of Virginia, among her friends and relatives. He was suddenly aware that she must have been quite apprehensive about meeting, really meeting, his family and friends. At that thought he frowned unconsciously. In the morning he would be taking her over to Ferry Farm to meet his mother.

Fittingly enough the next day was bleak and chill. The sun hovered behind sooty gray clouds, and a cold spring wind whined against the carriage. George sat beside Patsy, peering out the window morosely. The landscape looked bleak and forbidding, the familiar fields seemed barren. Strange how he, who loved land, could feel diminished by simply being present here. But, of course, that had to do with the frustrations of life with his mother, the restlessness of his adolescence before Lawrence rescued him by inviting him to Mount Vernon.

He was so deep in thought that he didn't feel Patsy's tentative slipping of her hand into his, nor was he aware when she withdrew it. Her anxious glances were lost on him, nor did he realize that she suddenly straightened up in the seat and pulled slightly away from him. He was taking her to meet his mother for the first time and suddenly he had become a stranger himself to her. It never occurred to him that Patsy might be wondering if he was less than proud to introduce his bride to his parent.

The carriage stopped at the farmhouse and he got out quickly. Still acting mechanically, he lifted Patsy down and putting one large hand under her elbow steered her up the stairs. For a moment she glanced up at him beseechingly, but at his brusque, "Come along," she looked straight ahead.

In the years since he had lived at Mount Vernon, he'd been home only for brief visits. Now he really looked at the house as an unfamiliar servant opened the door. The man's face was sullen, a typical expression for his mother's help, and George nodded to him briefly. The center hall had changed little. The family ate every meal there yet no single effort had ever been made to give the chamber a feeling of warmth or coziness or soothing atmosphere so essential to a dining room. It was still bleak, still cluttered with miscellaneous furniture that seemed to have been merely dropped in place rather than grouped with any eye to comfort or beauty.

So like his mother not to be waiting to meet them. "Where is Mrs. Washington?" George asked the servant.

"She be right down, sir. She say go into the parlor. She just finishing dressing."

Just like her. She hated dressing up and undoubtedly had started her toilette just as the carriage came into sight. He remembered the warm welcome he received from Patsy's mother, the courteous and friendly atmosphere of her home.

Patsy was still standing quietly but now her glance was thoughtful and questioning. He could not know that she was realizing that she was being introduced to another part of the complex man whom she'd married. Sometimes she had wondered why he spoke so seldom about Ferry Farm. Really all he had said was that this land was his inheritance from his father, but since he would a thousand times rather live on Mount Vernon, it suited him well for his mother to continue to occupy the house which was now his.

Small wonder that he had no desire to live in this bleak, forbidding home. Then he said, "Since our hostess is not prepared to receive us, shall we sit in here, my dear?"

Obediently she let him guide her into the small parlor off the hall. She spotted the book on the table, and trying to fill the uncomfortable silence, she walked over to it. It was the copy of *Contemplations,* which had been a fixture in this room for more than forty years.

Patsy opened to the first page and saw the two signatures there. George explained them. "My father, as you know, was a widower when he married my mother. The housekeeper resented the second marriage, and when my mother was carried into this room as a bride, the book was open to this page—with her predecessor's signature. As you can see, she lost no time in signing her own name with something of a large hand."

They both stared at the widely spaced letters that spelled out "Mary Ball Washington." And they both jumped when a penetrating voice from behind them said, "And I would advise any person beginning a marriage in which he is the second partner of the spouse to establish her—or his—presence with equal vigor."

George felt a deep flush come over his face as he drank in the unbelievable statement. This—his mother's greeting to him and his bride.

He turned around. His mother had dressed for them. He recognized the best lace cap, somewhat in need of pressing, the black silk dress she considered her finest.

He struggled with the familiar overwhelming anger at his mother's tactless statement, as pity fought the stronger emotion. His mother looked smaller, frailer. "Madame," he said lamely. Mechanically he reached down and kissed her cheek. He drew Patsy forward. "This is Mrs. Washington." He could have bitten his tongue at the formal introduction. "I mean, Mother, this is Patsy—Martha, that is."

Was it possible for a man to make such a fool of himself? he wondered miserably. Was he not to be spared a single one of the old emotions or would he run the entire gamut? So far in the last half hour he'd felt depressed, frustrated, annoyed, angry, and now downright stupid.

But, as usual, Patsy was equal to any situation. She seemed not to have heard his mother's opening statement as she extended both hands to the older woman and kissed her cheek warmly. Her greeting certainly conveyed more genuine pleasure at the meeting than his own had, George reflected, but at least the atmosphere in the room thawed out a little.

They sat down—oh, the remembered discomfort of these horsehair chairs—and his mother sent for tea. He knew that she was glad to see them. Her hand was even trembling just a bit. But his mother would tolerate no weakness or emotion in herself. He watched as she firmly clasped her hands in her lap and studied Patsy carefully.

Obviously she could find no fault with her. She gave a grudging nod of her head and turned to her son. "May I hope that you're finished with the army foolishness?"

"I believe you know I have resigned from the militia, Mother," George replied quietly. Furiously he reminded himself that this visit would last a very short time and he must not display anger here, not here of all places.

"Resigned." The word was a snort. "Far better you'd

never enlisted. Ill all that time—dysentery has been the death of many a stronger and better man than you—wasting your time, letting your land run down. It's a miracle you came out of it all. Poor Lawrence didn't know what he'd brought back inside him, and it killed him well after his fancy battles."

Had she really always been like this? George wondered.

"I am quite well, I assure you."

Patsy leaned forward in her chair. "I believe the tea is being served." For an instant her hand rested on his, then she withdrew it. Comforted, he resolved not to let his mother upset him.

The tea had not been brewed long enough. It was weak, and the cakes were soggy. Miserably George sipped while his mother complained about the incapable help she had to put up with.

Patsy tried to divert her. "The children and I are looking forward to Mount Vernon so much."

"Not much to look forward to from what I hear the way it's been neglected."

What was this awful need of his mother's to run down every achievement, every hope? But Patsy determinedly ignored the comment. "We shall have a fine time putting it to rights. Quite frankly I enjoy settling a new home very much. I'm quite happy that I'll have the chance to help with Mount Vernon. It would be a disappointment if it were complete now."

"Then there'll be no disappointment!" Mrs. Washington looked at her new daughter-in-law speculatively. "Betty tells me you have two fine homes already."

"The Custis homes are very pleasant." Patsy seemed to suspect what was coming.

"Well, my son is fortunate. His father was always land-poor. Always buying, adding a piece here, a piece there. We've got enough, I used to say. There's more to life than land."

George rose quietly. "And land, properly tended, can give back tenfold everything that is either needed or wanted. Mother, I think we must start. We will be setting off early tomorrow morning."

For a moment there was an unfathomable expression in her eyes, not tears, surely, but a touch of wistfulness, a yearning out. What did she want of him? Why could they not be closer? Why did he become withdrawn and formal in her presence? Why did she try forever and always to bait him? He bent down and touched her cheek with his lips.

In the carriage on the way back to Betty's he turned to Patsy. "Well?" But she was lost in thought. How could he ever have become what he was in that household? she wondered. Where under the sun had he managed to develop leadership qualities, faith in his own judgment, ability to make decisions when no single aspect of his career, no single accomplishment was given praise?

Praise? His mother didn't know the meaning of the word.

Tenderness? God help us all! Could Mary Washington always have been like that with her son? And yet it was so obvious that she did love him, was proud of him. Why, in heaven's name, had she never let herself say so?

Patsy felt sudden compassion for the lonely boy who used to escape to Mount Vernon. She reached for his hand, pressed it between both of hers, and raised it to her lips. "My poor old man," she murmured.

Her words shattered his feeling of depression. Suddenly he felt like a boy out of school. The visit he had feared was over. With infinite tenderness, infinite gratitude, he put his arms around Patsy and no longer noticed the bleak and depressing landscape of Ferry Farm.

A T Ferry Farm it had seemed as though winter was holding its tight grip on the land, but a few days later, as the carriage got near the Potomac country, spring seemed to line the road, to bid them welcome. Overnight the countryside became a riot of color; the grass lost its dry brown appearance and became a rich fertile green; the sun shone benevolently in the cloudless sky.

Everyone reacted to the excitement brought on by the nearness to Mount Vernon and the brilliant weather. Bishop muttered on every possible occasion, "Sure gonna be good to get home, Colonel, sure gonna be fine."

The children kept putting their heads out the window of the coach to see the unfamiliar area. Jacky constantly called to George, "Are we almost there, Poppa?" and even gentle little Patsy bounced up and down on the carriage seat, ignoring her mother's attempts to make her nap.

George found that he had to make a distinct effort to keep from galloping. As it was, every little while he would unconsciously press his knees into the side of his mount and the obedient animal would quicken his gait only to be immediately reined in.

Underneath his seemingly imperturbable calm, George was suffering the agonies of a housewife about to receive important company. Mentally he reviewed the layout of Mount Vernon. Was there anything he had forgotten? He'd sent a messenger on ahead with instructions to Alton to air the house, polish the furniture, and put up the beds. He'd also told the man to see about having food in for them.

The key was at Belvoir. Surely when Sally and George William knew he was coming, they'd ride over to check the house for him. He could count on them. He hadn't seen Sally in months, not since his last quick trip to Mount Vernon before the wedding. Would Patsy like Sally and would the two women become friends? They were so different, but it was important that they establish a friendship. A great part of the joy of life at Mount Vernon was based in the close ties with his Potomac neighbors and the most important of these were the Fairfaxes.

Finally they were on his land. A gentle wind rustled the trees that were already beginning to line the path to Mount Vernon. George restrained the impulse to ride ahead; as anxious as he was to see if all was in readiness, he wanted to share that first moment with Patsy. He rode next to the coach as they rounded the bend and came in view of the house. It had a freshly painted look as it sparkled white over the green grass that sloped gently down to the Potomac. The windows gleamed like diamonds and George smiled proudly. Mount Vernon looked like a beautiful woman just beginning to dress for a ball and quite confident of the ultimate effect of her appearance.

He had neither doubt nor hesitation when he looked at Patsy, whose shining eyes and eager smile told him she understood.

The house servants, starched and polished, immaculately dressed in the Washington livery, were waiting on the porch. Standing in front of them were Sally and George William. Their smiles were as joyful and radiant as he felt his own to be. Quickly he dismounted, opened the door of the carriage, and lifted Patsy down. The children tumbled out behind her as Bishop rushed to steady them.

"Welcome home, Colonel. Welcome home, Mrs. Washington." A chorus of voices cried the greeting as the slaves who worked in the house bobbed into curtsies or bowed.

Sally and George William held back an instant, seeming to want them to have this first moment unshared. Then they hurried forward together. Sally's kiss of greeting was a sisterly peck on his cheek and she immediately turned to Patsy. "We are so happy that you are here," she said.

Patsy's eyes held a hint of tears. "I have looked forward to meeting you both."

George was aware that Sally looked more beautiful than ever, that, at twenty-nine, dignity and sophistication were fulfilling her girlish loveliness. The realization brought no regret and he was so proud of the way Patsy was handling this meeting. She looked serene and well-groomed as she greeted his friends and his servants, and showed no signs of being fatigued from the tiresome, dusty ride.

Sally said, "We're going to join you in a few minutes but I've arranged for luncheon and do want to see that everything is ready. We'll talk later." Without giving them a chance to answer, she and George William slipped away to go to the kitchen house. With their exquisite tact the Fairfaxes were letting the Washingtons have their first moments in their home alone.

George was delighted to see that inside the house George William had faithfully tried to follow the many instructions that had been rushed to him. The furniture shone with the effort of high polishing. The floors had been sanded and the tester bedstead had been installed in the downstairs bedroom. He'd ordered the room painted and papered in blue and white and the effect was pleasing. As Jacky and little Patsy scampered up the stairs to investigate their new rooms, he showed Patsy through the house, flooding her with details about the changes he'd already made and how much more they would be doing.

She listened, asked questions, paused to delight over the new coverlet, the curtains, the view from the bedroom.

The table had been set for the meal and George was pleased to see that the new china and glasses had arrived. In a little while Sally and George William joined them. The four sat down at the table with the children. Sally had ordered the meal, but it was Patsy who rang the bell to indicate when more dishes were to be brought in and who directed that tea be served. It was Patsy who immediately became the hostess.

With half his mind George kept up an animated conversation with George William about the state of the plantation, asking his friend for any information about what matters needed attention first. But he was able to follow the womanly chatter between Patsy and Sally. Patsy was telling Sally about the wedding and all the festivities in Williamsburg. He heard Patsy say that she had never enjoyed dancing very much until this season but George was such a superb partner that he made her feel quite graceful and accomplished. A wave of nostalgia swept over him as Sally said quietly, "Yes, I know."

The children left the table early, but when the Fairfaxes were about to leave, they came back to say good-bye. Little Patsy had a delicate flush of color on her cheeks. She put her arm around her stepfather's knee and George picked her up. "Tell us how you like your new home," he instructed the little girl.

Jacky answered for her. "Oh, Poppa, we like it very much. And I heard Bishop say you'll be riding before breakfast tomorrow morning to see all the fields. And I thought I could go with you and help."

George William burst out laughing. "I haven't heard a finer offer of assistance in all my days," he said, tousling Jacky's head. "And if you have any spare time, young man, perhaps you'll lend me a hand over at Belvoir."

There was a tinge of sadness in Sally's voice as she said to the children, "When Poppa and Mamma come to visit, you must be sure to come, too. I have many toys at Belvoir for our nieces and nephews."

George understood the meaning behind the sadness. There was little probability that after ten years of marriage Sally would ever have a child to grow up in Belvoir. She and George William had always seemed to have everything. Now, beginning his life in Mount Vernon as a married man, he had a feeling that the balance had shifted. The social life of the Potomac families would be centered here rather than at Belvoir. He would no longer be riding to the Fairfaxes' to escape the loneliness of his home. Rather, these two beloved friends at the threshold of the end of youth would be coming here. Just as they had filled his needs for so long, he and Patsy might be able to help fill theirs.

He accompanied them outside and down the steps to where a groom was waiting with their horses. Quietly he lifted Sally onto hers.

"Thank you, young Washington," she smiled, then said, "Oh, dear, I think I'd better not call you that any-more—now that you're properly married and the head of a family."

"Patsy calls me her old man," George replied.

George William burst into laughter. "And, by heaven, when you're in one of your serious moods, it's a name that suits you well." He leaned down and held out his hand. "It's been a fine day."

George shook the hand vigorously and turned with his own still outstretched, to offer Sally. But she was holding her riding crop in one hand, the reins in the other. For a single instant she stared at him with an unfathomable expression in her green eyes. Then she brought the crop sharply against the side of her mount.

"Race you home, darling," she cried and started down the path. Laughing, George William dug his spurs into his horse and galloped behind her. George watched as they streaked out of sight. How many times had he been part of those mad races across the fields and over fences to the steps of Belvoir.

A feeling of chill and loneliness came over him. He hurried inside, looking for Patsy. But she was upstairs, supervising the children's baths and did not hear when he called her.

THE EXECUTIVE MANSION AT PHILA-
delphia had a disembodied look. At last the
great crates were out of the hall and packed into the supply carriages. At last the endless debate about which of
the personal furniture to have returned to Mount Vernon
and which to discard was over.

It was decided to bring Nelly's bedstead back home.
Nelly had indicated a certain desire for a new, more
fashionable bed but had been firmly refused by her
grandmother. The trundle for under the bed was being
kept, too. George understood the reason for that. Long
ago little Patsy had curled up to nap there.

The large mirrors they had brought to Philadelphia
were a problem. They needed to be crated with absolute
care. Some of the roads they'd be driving over were rough
and bumpy. A badly packaged mirror would arrive in
smithereens.

During the week of packing it seemed to George
that never did fifteen minutes go by before a caller came

to offer one last farewell. In despair, he finally told Lear to simply put all the papers in boxes, and they'd worry about sorting them at home. Not, God knows, that he expected too much leisure at Mount Vernon. With growing alarm he kept track of the number of people who insisted they'd be down to Mount Vernon for a real visit shortly. With spring about to break he had every reason to believe that most of them were sincere.

That thought led him to order new carpeting for the blue room. The last time he'd been home he'd realized how badly it was needed. He wondered if age could possibly be bringing on irritability. A hundred times during that last week he firmly closed his lips over sharp words. But it was so damnable and infuriating to see precious possessions being carelessly crated. He didn't intend to arrive home with carriages filled with battered belongings.

Nelly had a pair of parrots. Their squawking sent shivers through George and he'd hoped that she would leave them in Philadelphia. He'd even gone out of his way to suggest to some friends that they volunteer to take the birds. Apparently his hints had been too subtle. Nelly carefully planned minute details of the parrots' traveling arrangements.

Young Washington sincerely tried to be helpful. George received many suggestions from the lad, most of which were impractical. It was a relief to him when the boy went off to make his own farewells to the young ladies and then returned to Princeton. He'd be just like his father. That thought brought a wry smile. The Custis boys were handsome and charming. A little less charm would have been a blessing.

Young Lafayette was in a troubled state and no one could blame him. Every ship from France brought new rumors, but it did seem likely that the Marquis would be released from prison soon. The boy had worried so long about his family and George knew that he wished he were sharing their imprisonment. Often he reminded his ward that he was the hope of continuity of a great French name, that his father's one consolation in the past five years had been the knowledge that he was safe. Now that the strain was almost over, the young son of the French nobleman was showing the effect of it. He, too, would be better off in Virginia. The countryside in the spring could not help but relieve and soothe any spirit.

Patsy had come down with a heavy cold. Her colds frightened him terribly. The doctors had warned that any inflammation of bronchial tubes would almost surely go into pneumonia. He'd tried to forbid her to leave her bed, but she wouldn't listen to him. Trying not to cough, she'd insisted that what they both needed was to get home and get settled, and she'd be absolutely fine once they were back where they belonged.

The morning of departure was windy and cold. Naturally, George told himself sardonically. It had been folly to hope for a balmy day in March. He ordered that extra robes be put in the chariot. Patsy had to be protected from drafts. He wanted to ride in his phaeton but didn't even suggest it. Time enough for that if the weather improved a bit, and Patsy would be fretting about his throat if he rode in an open vehicle today.

They had a last breakfast in the dining room. The staff servants, who would be staying on with the Adamses, were grim-faced and quiet. The Mount Vernon servants had an attitude of barely concealed excitement. Patsy barely touched her breakfast but George insisted she have a second cup of hot tea. To his discerning eye it seemed that her eyes were overly bright, almost feverish.

Anxiety over her made it easy to get away. He felt no lingering or regret now. The farewells had been said. Finally he and Patsy got into the main carriage. They pulled away promptly at 7 A.M.

Nelly yawned behind her hand. "Oh, it's such a bitter day," she sighed. "Do you think spring will ever come?"

Patsy had a glint of amusement in her expression. "If you think today is cold, you should have known a few of the winters we experienced. I can remember riding to join Grandpapa when the bitter cold literally caked the horses' breath."

"But Grandmama always came," George said. "How we waited for her carriage to pull up. Not one of these overloaded vehicles can begin to compare with the way hers was packed with ham and cakes and wines and preserves. The news that Mrs. Washington was coming to camp made every man in the army rejoice. I think they felt that the commander was in far better disposition when his lady was about."

"I can remember you packing for those trips," Nelly said. "Remember the trunk that you always used, Grandmama? You told me we used to cry when you packed it in the fall but joyfully helped you unpack after your return in the spring. I do remember that sometimes you'd be crying then because you worried about Grandpapa when the spring campaigns started."

Patsy blushed a deep crimson and George smiled. "Your grandmama never hinted she was worried. She insisted that I and my army were invincible. She really made me believe it, too."

"I always did believe it," Patsy said firmly. "And I recall doing very little weeping."

She felt her husband's sharp glance and knew he was thinking of the same thing that was going through her mind—the endless weeping she had done after that first terrible grief came to Mount Vernon . . .

A FTER A LONG, HARD WINTER AND A late spring summer burst forth on the Potomac. The tulip trees and magnolias, the violets, the catalpa, and the New Scotland spruce vied with each other to drench the land in color. The weeping willows had many boughs broken and bent from the weight of the winter snows, but the kitchen gardens were filled with currants and raspberries and great quantities of peaches and cherries.

In fourteen years of uninterrupted life at Mount Vernon George had succeeded in fulfilling many of his early dreams for the mansion and grounds. His original inheritance had included two thousand acres and the house. Now the boundaries of the plantation covered over six thousand acres and he had options on other nearby property.

He had added to the main house and the surrounding buildings before he and Patsy had married, but now together they were about to begin the addition that he had always wanted. Construction was going to start on two wings, one at either end of the main building. One of those wings would consist of a combination dining room and ballroom. The other would have a library with a private staircase over it leading to a new suite for him and Patsy.

The additions were necessary. On that first night when he'd brought Patsy home, he had had an insight into the fact that Mount Vernon would become a social mecca. How very right he'd been! Indeed he often felt that he operated a hotel and should put his occupation down as innkeeper.

It wasn't just the many neighbors and friends along the Potomac who came. His brothers, his sister Betty, the dozens of assorted nieces and nephews, the friends Jacky brought home from school, the young girls and cousins who clustered around little Patsy—together they made for an endless array of parties and socials and merry evenings of singing and music in the parlor.

Often he sighed for a quiet night and knew the wish to be dishonest. He enjoyed the young people just as much as Patsy did and was unceasingly amazed at the quiet efficiency with which she kept the great house constantly shining and the meals constantly delicious, no matter how great the strain on her hospitality.

Just as he had expected, Sally and George William came to Mount Vernon more than he and Patsy went to

Belvoir. Fourteen years had not removed the merry twinkle from Sally's eyes. She sometimes lamented her thinness, sighing over the fact that it made for lines and wrinkles, but George never found her less attractive than that long-ago day when he'd first seen her on the staircase at Belvoir.

Once he had feared that attraction, but now he welcomed it. The knowledge that Sally and George William were to be guests for dinner gave a sense of anticipation to his whole day. She could still amuse him and challenge him. She would forever be his favorite dancing partner, although he took care never to dance with her too often at any ball. But the deep measure of his happiness and contentment abided in his life with Patsy. All these years she had soothed and filled the restless, unvoiced yearning that he could still remember from youth and young manhood.

Once he had been intrigued by the almost offhand grace with which Sally ran Belvoir. Now he couldn't imagine having completed all the plans for Mount Vernon if Patsy had not been as caring and concerned as he. How many nights had he spent hours thinking aloud, talking about the wisdom of assuming yet another mortgage to add to the property, or going into debt with the London agents to purchase draperies or carpeting or fixtures. Always her opinion had been a verification of what he wanted to do; always she had helped assume the responsibility for an expenditure that might result in a need for economy; always she had shown her total faith in his judgment.

In every way except one—in all these years Patsy had never really allowed him to share in raising her children. George knew his wife would have been astonished at that thought. She always consulted him on every detail of the minor decisions about Jacky and Patsy. But in a major crisis if there was a choice between what he felt was right and what the children wanted, his opinion was always discarded.

Once he had hoped that when more children were born, he would be able to share fully in the joys of parenthood. But Patsy had had no child of his. That second winter after their marriage she had been very ill. Maybe that was the reason for their lack of issue. Sometimes George wondered why neither his home nor Belvoir had been blessed with an heir. He comforted himself with the knowledge that the Almighty had reasons for the slightest occurrence in human lives. Surely the Almighty had had a reason for this all-important withholding.

He knew that he had transferred the love he might have offered his own offspring to little Patsy and Jacky. His wife would always be first in his life and indeed that would have been true even if he had had a houseful of heirs. But after her, her children were dearest to him.

George accepted the fact that he was human enough to resent Patsy's blindness to his feelings. He admitted to himself that she put her children's welfare before his. But they were growing up rapidly and soon, in all probability, would be embarking on lives of their own.

When Jacky turned eighteen, it was quite obvious that he was in something of a rush to take on adult responsibilities. George managed to pluck him from a romantic entanglement in one school and get him settled in King's College. Then to his disgust Jacky met Nellie Calvert and promptly proposed. His mother reacted with mixed pleasure to the announcement, but George was dismayed and angered. He had nothing against Nellie, who was a fine and pretty girl, but Jacky needed to keep his mind on his schooling. He was showing signs of turning into an irresponsible lighthead, and in a few years he'd be in control of a large fortune. He should achieve maturity before sealing his future.

George could not prevent the early engagement, but he did make it quite plain to Nellie's father that he would not hear of marriage until Jacky had completed his college education, which would take nearly four years. Jacky went back to school, seemingly satisfied with the arrangement, and Nellie came to Mount Vernon for a long visit.

One June morning shortly after her arrival George got up with an unexpectedly lighthearted feeling. It seemed to him that just as summer had burst forth overnight, so many of the nagging issues of the past year had been resolved. Nellie was a delightful girl and perhaps the engagement would keep Master Custis from too much socializing with other young ladies. As long as the marriage was delayed until his graduation, George was even willing to concede that perhaps the engagement might be a steadying influence in Jacky's life.

During the past year George had been worried about another matter, too. More clearly than many, he understood the grave implications of the growing hostility between the Colonies and England. Many times, he had wondered if the breach was widening too rapidly to be healed. But on the morning of June 19 as he looked out the window and observed his long-desired English country garden, he would not let himself believe that in the end the differences would not be settled.

He knew he hadn't changed too much since the days of his military command. Oh, granted, his hair now had a little gray and the lines around his mouth had deepened, but he still felt as physically fit as he had a generation ago. One couldn't be outdoors most of the day and run to fat or flab.

Patsy came in from her dressing room, smoothing the lace edging on the collar of her morning dress. He smiled at her. "Mrs. Washington looks very fine indeed."

Her laugh was rueful. "Mrs. Washington is remembering when she was only slightly slimmer than her daughter is now. George, she really does seem better don't you think?"

"I do, most certainly." George wished the hearty reassurance in his voice were honest. At sixteen little Patsy was the beauty of the county. She had the dark Custis hair and the chiseled profile of that handsome family. She had never lost the touch of wistfulness that had endeared her to him that long-ago afternoon in the Chamberlayn parlor, and she had never become any stronger than she was in those baby days when her mother fretted so terribly about her health.

Little Patsy was still frail. Her frightening spells came too easily. There were too many parties that she could not attend. Too often they started out for a festive day and returned home because she had slumped over, exhausted and trembling.

George thought of the countless times he had carried her up to her room after those spells, of the way she would cling to him and the frightened way she would finally whisper, "I think I'm all right now, Poppa." In the past weeks there had been fewer of these attacks. But much as he might try to comfort her mother with heartiness and optimism, he himself was constantly worried about his stepdaughter.

Still, he realized that his sense of optimism on this morning was extending to include Patsy's health. "She is most certainly improving," he repeated firmly, "and before long, I have no doubt, I'll be playing the role of the stern parent when the first young man requests her hand."

"Oh, she must not marry too young," Patsy cried. "I won't have it. It's all right for Jacky but she's not ready for that kind of thing yet."

"In heaven's name, what is that kind of thing?" George asked, and his laugh joined hers as they started for the dining room.

Nellie Calvert was already at her place at the table. Pretty Nellie was obviously still living in a world peopled only by herself and Master Custis. Her greeting was to say that Jacky had described just such mornings as this and how much he enjoyed a ride along the Potomac before breakfast.

George ignored the implication of how wonderful it would be if Jacky were home now. God knows there wasn't the slightest chance of making a scholar of the boy, but he had to have some schooling and discipline if he were to manage properly his very large inheritance.

Little Patsy came into the dining room. Her skirts rustled as she bent down to kiss her mother. Then her arms went around his neck. "Good morning, Poppa," she murmured as she kissed his ear.

He looked at her closely. She had good color and her eyes were sparkling. Her blue gown reflected in the caramel color of her eyes. "How pretty we are this morning," he commented. "Did you sleep well, darling?"

"So soundly I might have been dead," little Patsy laughed. But somehow the words sent a chill through him.

Nellie's young friend, who was also visiting Mount Vernon, joined them, and George commented that he rarely had the pleasure of breakfasting with three such lovely young ladies. At Patsy's raised eyebrow he corrected himself quickly. "Four such lovely young ladies," he said as they all laughed.

After breakfast he was glad to excuse himself and go out to the fields. It was obvious that the conversation was going to be on future wedding plans and gowns and slippers. With the wedding four years away he envisioned many such conversations in the months to come.

When he returned home, he was delighted to find his brother Jack there with his wife, Hannah, and two of their offspring. George greeted his brother affectionately, his wife with an unconscious touch of reserve. He suspected the unannounced visit was not for the joy of seeing him and Patsy but because Jack's wife wanted to get a good look at Nellie Calvert. She knew that he and Patsy were concerned over the quick engagement.

But still, it was a pleasant and happy afternoon,

made even more so by the fact that little Patsy appeared to be in better health and spirits than she had been for a long time.

At four o'clock when they left the table, she went to her room to get a letter she had received from Jacky at college. Soon after, she was seized with one of her usual fits and collapsed. It was Nelly who heard her fall.

It wasn't like one of little Patsy's usual spells, when she became flushed and shaken. This time she was so quiet, so still, her breathing scarcely was discernible. Her life was like a frail candle in a ferocious wind. One single movement might snuff it out.

With infinite care, George picked her up and lifted her onto the bed. Patsy frantically called for help, but he had seen death too often to be deceived. He sank to his knees beside the bed, took little Patsy's hand in his and, with tears running down his cheeks, his voice broken with sobs, began to recite the prayers for the dying.

In less than two minutes, she was gone. His tears fell on the curls that clustered on her forehead as he kissed her and rose to his feet. Patsy, her face gray with anxiety, reached for her daughter's hands and began rubbing them. Then, realizing that little Patsy was no longer breathing, she looked imploringly at him.

He took his wife in his arms as her first anguished sob broke against his chest. He nodded to the others.

"Leave us alone," he commanded quietly. When the door closed behind them, he began to cradle Patsy's head against his shoulder, but with a shriek, she slipped out of his embrace and threw herself across the still form on the bed.

IN THE WEEKS THAT FOLLOWED THE DEATH, George tried every device to lift Patsy from her deep depression. His own heart ached sorely for the gentle girl whom he had loved so dearly, but he never even contemplated his own loss as he spent every possible moment trying to distract the grieving mother.

He enlisted the help of the Fairfaxes and nearly every day Sally arrived with a tempting dish from Belvoir to try to induce Patsy to eat. Sally, being Sally, could always manage to cheer and George watched with gratitude as slowly but skillfully she planted the thought that little Patsy had died at a joyous time in her life, before she became a real invalid, before she had to face the painful knowledge that her ailment would have precluded marriage and children.

When Patsy spoke of the tragedy of her child's lifelong poor health, Sally would counter with a dozen happy memories of parties and dances when little Patsy, beautiful in a new gown, had been the center of attention. She would reminisce over the girl's joy in her pony and the wonderful surprises that were always in the boxes from

England. "Sometimes she would weep when she was ill," Sally said, "but in all the years I never once saw her weep because she was unhappy. I used to think that if we had been blessed with a daughter, I should have wanted to give her so much happiness."

George William would often come over at the end of the day to accompany Sally home. He seemed to understand George's feelings and wordlessly managed to convey a sympathy that was a balm to George's troubled spirit.

One evening, nearly a month after the death, they were having a glass of wine together in the study and George William said matter-of-factly, "It is hard for you, too. How I used to envy you the adoration of that pretty child. Well, they say a father is naturally attracted to a daughter and she to him."

"And what do they say about a stepfather?" George asked bitterly, then could have bitten his tongue over the words.

George William shot him a look of sympathy. "I would guess that most people would say that a stepfather probably knows the same pain of loss as a natural father, but will never be credited with it. But time is a remedy for everything—for grief, for lack of understanding."

George slowly turned the stem of the wineglass and stared at it. "I am afraid that the remedy for my wife's grief is to bring her son home from college. She seems to feel that with Jacky here she will be able to bear her loss. You see, Jacky, being a Custis, can truly share her sorrow."

"If Jacky leaves college now, he'll never go back." George William's words were a statement that left no room for discussion.

"No, he won't," George agreed. "But his mother feels that it might be well for him to marry soon. Then there will be grandchildren for her to help raise. She is already saying that when Nellie and Jacky marry she would like them to live here or build a home nearby. But if Jacky wants to reside on one of the Custis plantations, she can always visit them often."

George William put his glass down, came over, and touched his shoulder briefly.

George looked up with a grateful smile. "You realize there isn't another person I would discuss this with. And yet, who knows, it may be all right in time. These are simply troubled days on every level."

"On one level I believe that all will be well eventually," George William said. "Patsy will come out of her grief and turn to you. You must give her time. But on the level of the Colonies and England I'm very much afraid that we are sailing on a disaster course."

"Which makes it harder and harder for you." George knew how difficult the political climate was for George

William. As the possible heir of Lord Fairfax he was caught in the crossfire of antagonism between England and the Colonies.

"Well, by the time we return it will probably all be over with and resolved." Then, as George stared at him apprehensively, George William walked over to the fireplace and leaned an elbow against the mantel. "We have decided to live in England," he said. "As you know, my future expectations are completely dependent upon my relations with my family there. The separation of miles often causes an emotional separation. Then too I hope to get some treatment at Bath for this arthritis before it gets too much worse."

George had known that someday the Fairfaxes would go to England and perhaps even reside there. But it was unthinkable to lose them now.

"How soon do you contemplate leaving?" he asked.

"In a few weeks. I was about to tell you last month when . . . when the tragedy occurred, and I haven't wanted to bring it up since then. But now I must."

George thought of the twenty-five years that had passed since he and George William went on that first surveying trip and came back fast friends. Over the years they'd traded tools and horses, argued politics, hunted together, and spent countless evenings in each other's homes. The thought of losing this great friend and

Sally . . . and Sally . . . brought an ache almost as final as the one caused by little Patsy's death.

"These are indeed sad times," he said heavily. "You only tell me now that you are going and I find my mind leaping to the happy day, perhaps years away, when you shall return."

George William nodded. "If there is one single consolation in this move, it is that we will be removed from the position of having to take sides for or against the mother country. In England, I will be able to be a reasonable voice in high circles speaking for the cause of the colonists. Here I am too ill to fight for the Colonies, if fighting should come, and I would be forced to alienate either family or friends by taking sides. Soon it will be impossible to speak a moderate word for England in America. But in England, I believe I can be a colonist demanding for my countrymen their rights as Englishmen.

George said, "Yes, a few genteel voices, speaking for us, cutting through the belief that we are crude barbarians rather than Englishmen, might make a great difference."

George William went to the decanter and refilled both their glasses. He raised his in what was almost a toast. "Long ago I made a prophecy that you would become a great military leader. I was right then. Now I make another prophecy that if this rebellion becomes a full-scale revolution, you will be chosen to lead it."

"I have no desire to lead a revolution," George protested. "God knows I would seek no such task."

"Nevertheless, you will be given that task. Prepare yourself and your affairs, George. I see it coming."

"What do you see coming?" Sally was at the doorway. She looked tired and shadows made her green eyes seem even larger. "Patsy has gone to sleep. I think her spirits are a little better tonight," she told George, then repeated her question. "What do you see coming?"

"I see our friend here called back to lead the military," George William replied.

Sally nodded. "Remember, long ago, I told you that George had the mark of greatness. And you both laughed."

"I remember very keenly," George smiled. "I believe we laughed because your spouse was expecting a prediction of quite another sort—something about a new carriage."

Sally shook her head. "My, young Washington, you do have a keen memory. Now, even in this very unhappy time, I wish to make a prophecy of my own. The sadness will pass and your greatness will be known. I believe it."

George looked at her steadily. "And when do you foretell that the Fairfaxes of Belvoir will return from England?"

There was a sudden rush of tears in her eyes. Biting her lip, she turned from him and reached for the glass of wine that George William was holding out to her.

"I don't know," she said. "I just don't know."

A few weeks later Patsy went with him to accompany the Fairfaxes to the ferry that would take them on the first stage of their long journey. George William clasped his hand vigorously, then grabbed his shoulders in a brief hug. Sally's tear-stained kiss lingered against his cheek. Then they were tiny toylike figures waving determinedly as the ferry vanished from sight.

Patsy waved her handkerchief, then dabbed her eyes with it. "So many good-byes," she sighed, "so many." The family doctor and longtime friend, Dr. Craik, had accompanied them and was standing off a little way. He eyed Patsy sharply but apparently found no cause for comment.

Wordlessly the three went back to the carriage. As they pulled away from the landing slip, George had a sensation of total loss and depression. He was sure he would never again see Sally and George William. Was it possible that the happy days were completely behind him? These last fourteen years had been very, very happy. Was life henceforth to be only a comparison to a life that was finished?

He stirred restlessly. No, a chapter was finished but not their lives. He would get on with the additions to Mount Vernon. Working again on the plans would surely give him a sense of accomplishment and purpose.

If Patsy wanted to allow an early marriage between

Jacky and Nellie, he wouldn't fight it any longer. Something positive had to be done to relieve her grief. If that relief would only come when she could focus her love and attention on a new generation of the Custis family, then so be it.

In the coming months it would be important that Patsy find some cause for happiness. It would be too much for her to worry about the very real threat to the entire structure of their lives that was looming all over the Colonies.

Mr. O'Flynn's inn was called the "Sign of the Ship." George remembered it as a quiet place with good beds. As the retinue drew up to the establishment, he sincerely hoped that it had not changed in either way.

Stiff and tired, they got out of the carriage. The roads had been somewhat dryer and smoother than he'd dared expect, but still, it had been a long day, and the jolting and swaying of the coach had obviously fatigued Patsy. She could not hold back the coughing any longer as she stepped into the sharp wind.

He took her arm and hurried her inside, but to his dismay the inn seemed quite cold and drafty. The proprietor hurried to greet them and made an obsequious speech about how their presence warmed his heart.

But not your establishment, George thought grimly, and asked if the fire might not be stirred up. "Lady Washington is chilled. And kindly have the beds warmed

promptly. Lady Washington is fatigued from the journey. And . . .

"And Lady Washington is hungry," Patsy laughed. "Stop fussing, old man. I'll be fine."

Indeed she did look better when they were finally all at table and George relaxed somewhat when he realized that the cooking at this inn would make it worthwhile eating here in furs if necessary. But still, Patsy must not get chilled. She mustn't get sick—not now. He eyed her sharply every time she turned her head to cough. "You shall retire as soon as dinner is over," he ordered. "And if you are not much better tomorrow, we'll stay over another day."

"No such thing." Patsy shook her head vehemently. "The faster I get home, the sooner I'll be fine. The real solution would be to travel all night to get there more quickly."

George looked around the table. "Does anyone have any message for Philadelphia?" he asked. "I must write to Lear about some pamphlets I want him to purchase for me."

"Don't forget to inquire about the livery clothes." Patsy's tone gave no hint that he was supposed to have inquired about them before they left this morning.

"Sir, may I assist you in writing any notes?" Fred Frestal, young Lafayette's tutor, was a pleasant young man; his deferential offers of assistance were genuine and he did not make them unless he felt there was a fair chance of acceptance.

George smiled in appreciation. "Indeed if I had more than one page to write, I'd gladly accept aid, but my letter-writing will consist of no more than a few lines of instructions to the Philadelphia household."

"I have a line you can add, Grandpapa." Nelly's eyes danced even while her tone was somewhat hesitant. "It seems that something far more important than the livery was forgotten, something which would grieve you terribly to lose."

George laid down his fork. Nelly's eyes belied her words. "Pray inform me what we could possibly have left behind in all of Philadelphia that would cause me any grief," he said.

"I'll give you a hint," Nelly offered. "There are two of them. They are living creatures. The sounds emanating from them cheer your very soul. You love them so much that you wanted to share them with others."

"You forgot your parrots?" George asked incredulously. "After all the protestations of love about the things, and that you couldn't be parted a day from them. And you forgot them!"

"Not really," Nelly explained. "I was carrying them myself in their cage and then I laid the cage down for just a moment to run back to my room. I thought I'd forgotten my shawl. But I found that indeed I had my shawl and then I forgot to pick up the cage with the parrots. So you will ask Lear to be sure to bring them with him, won't you?"

George nodded. "My only regret is that I have not had the pleasure of knowing that the creatures were not part of our retinue today. It would have given me joy to realize they were safely stranded in Philadelphia."

"Oh, Grandpapa," Nelly protested.

Lafayette buttered a generous slice of bread. "Have you informed the general about the dog?" he asked Nelly slyly.

George put his fork down again and stared at his granddaughter. "Did we forget your dog? Or shall I say did you forget your dog?"

There was just the proper amount of rueful acknowledgment of error in Nelly's expression and voice. "I'm afraid it shared the fate of the parrots," she admitted.

Young Lafayette laughed outright; the tutor could not hide a discreet smile, and Patsy shook her head even while she tried to swallow a chuckle. George was unable to keep the corners of his mouth from twitching. Certainly no meal was dull with a young member of the Custis family present.

Later that evening after Patsy and the others had gone to bed, George wrote to Lear. He wrote about the mirrors and the livery clothes and the pamphlets. Then with a sigh, he added a postscript. "On one side I am called upon to remember the parrots; on the other to remember the dog. For my own part I would not pine much if all of them were forgotten."

They spent the second night in Elkton, the third in Harford. A heavy snowstorm greeted them as they approached Baltimore. The wind howled against the windows of the carriage and the thick white flakes swirled in the late afternoon light.

George shook his head. He knew that they were bound to have an escort going into Baltimore and he didn't want Patsy standing out in the cold to hear speeches.

"Why does it always seem as though the worst storm of all is just when spring is around the corner?" Nelly asked suddenly. "Somehow it seems wasteful and unnecessary."

"You mean that it shouldn't snow if there's a great possibility that it will all melt soon?" George asked.

"Something like that, I suppose," Nelly replied. "It's just that now I'm ready for spring and I really don't want to adjust to snow."

"There are many things in life you really don't want to adjust to," Patsy said mildly, "and I hope the worst of them is the weather."

"Oh I know, Grandmama," Nelly said, "and it really isn't even the snow itself. It's just that I'm afraid that if this becomes a blizzard we'll have to stay over a day and I hate to wait when I want something badly. And I do want to get home badly."

Patsy's smile turned into a deep cough. George watched her intently, but she quickly recovered. "You don't like waiting or delays. Then it's very fortunate you were not the commander in chief of the revolutionary forces twenty years ago," she told her granddaughter.

"Nor the commander's lady," George injected dryly. "Patsy, do you remember the snowstorms in those years? Did it seem that the heavens would ever show blue again?"

The sound of horses hooves approaching made them all peer out the windows of the carriage. "It must be the escort," George said, "and from the sound I take it to be a large one."

"Perfectly proper," Patsy said briskly. "There'll never be one large enough to honor you sufficiently." Then she laughed. "But we must admit that some of the greetings have been imaginative."

George laughed outright and Nelly looked perplexed. "Of course you mean the maidens and their mothers in Trenton—the reception they tendered me when I was on the way to the first Inauguration."

"Will you miss having an escort, Grandpapa?" Nelly asked. "I don't suppose you'll have one after we get home, will you?"

"After we get home, Farmer Washington will require no escort," George said fervently. "And I think Grandmama will not mind having an old man squire her about on her visits."

The Baltimore escort had come upon them. Through the driving snow they could see smartly garbed officers, rigidly upright on their mounts, fall into place to the front and rear of the carriages.

Nelly's eyes danced with excitement. "I confess it will be hard to get used to not having an escort," she said. "I've really been used to them for such a long time, ever since I was a little girl."

"At seventeen, eight years is a long time," Patsy agreed. "I was much older when I was first greeted and escorted by an official party. I remember I wrote to my friend Betsy Ramsey that one would think I was a very great somebody."

Automatically she began retying the strings of her bonnet, smoothing the hair that touched her forehead, straightening her cloak. "That was the first long trip I ever took in my life," she said to Nelly. "It was the first time I joined Grandpapa during the war. I went to Cambridge to be with him."

She folded her hands in her muff. "The papers called me, 'the lady of His Excellency.' I was quite nervous because when my carriage went through a town, so many people lined the curbs. I tried so hard not to let them see that I was quite terrified. But I think on that trip I really understood that if I was to be Grandpapa's wife, I would have to live up to him."

"You hadn't seen each other in such a long time," Nelly said. "How wonderful it must have been." Her eyes shone dreamily. "Someday when I love someone very much, I would not want to be separated from him ever. But if we were separated for a while, I think the reunion would be so wonderful."

George looked at Patsy. He was sure the same memories were flashing through her mind. His eyes twinkled as he said, "Oh, your grandmama and I had a very prosaic reunion. Within half an hour of her arrival she was sewing buttons on my uniform jacket."

"Buttons!" Nelly looked dismayed.

And to George's amusement the faintest trace of a blush could be seen on Patsy's cheek.

FTER THE FAIRFAXES LEFT, GEORGE tried to keep the schedule he had set for himself. In a state of compulsive energy he mapped out the timetable for the additions to the main house—the library and bedroom on the south and the ballroom on the north. Meticulously he laid out his plans and his exact instructions for each detail of the construction work, as though he already suspected that he would not be here to supervise the job himself.

No detail of the grounds or buildings escaped him. The kitchen house needed repairs. He had them completed. More spinning wheels and scythes were ordered and other tools and implements inspected. Preparation and foresight . . . Somehow he could not forget George William's warning.

The political situation became worse. George found that honor dictated he be an active participant in the breaking of ties with England. Cautiously he counseled the immediate training of the militia. He was a proponent of the day of fasting to dramatize protest at the closing of the Port of Boston.

Although he tried to spend every possible moment with Patsy after the Fairfaxes left, he always felt as though somehow she was closing him out, excluding him. Oh, he knew that it wasn't deliberate. But she continued to use expressions like, "if you could only understand . . ." He wrote to King's College, instructing them to send Jacky home even though he silently protested that his own presence and love should have been sufficient to sustain his wife. But there was no easing of her quiet weeping in the night until he agreed to write.

Her gratitude when he sent the letter was as much a rebuff as her hurt silence when he had tried to delay the homecoming. It was just that Jacky understood. He was little Patsy's brother . . . that was why she wanted to see him married . . . so that soon there would be children . . . maybe even a little girl who would look like little Patsy. George wondered where he fitted into the picture.

Yet, on the surface, life seemed smooth enough. There certainly was no visible sign of the rampant upheaval. There might be strain in the government but when the House of Burgesses met in Williamsburg, most of the members still attended the governor's ceremonial dinner.

If warfare came, Mount Vernon might well be a target for shelling from British vessels, but no one who witnessed the lavish outlay of money for additions would guess that fear.

He and Patsy might be near strangers, each becoming daily more absorbed in a special worry, a special grief, but that growing estrangement was not visible to the guests who filled Mount Vernon or the friends they visited.

In February of '74 Jacky and Nellie were married. Patsy would not go to the Calvert home in New Kent for the wedding. She was afraid that she would spoil it by weeping for the young girl who would not be there to be a bridesmaid. George went without her and tried to truly enter the festivities and not burden the young people with his continuing disapproval.

The fact of the wedding seemed to lift Patsy's spirits. She took a more active interest in the progress of the construction and listened more carefully to the talk she heard about a break with England.

The following September George went to Philadelphia as an elected delegate to the Continental Congress. He decided to go in military uniform, then faced the reality that one could not go to a congress that was convening to discuss possible war in the very uniform of the hostile side.

He chose instead the blue-and-red uniform worn during his service in the fight against the French and their Indian allies.

At that session in Philadelphia he was elected to command the county militia companies and the winter was spent in drilling and reviewing them. He was struck by the boyish faces of the eager recruits. He knew how they would harden and mature if war came. With a sense of near yearning he watched the clumsy awkwardness of some of them—youths who obviously had seldom handled a gun. But then the soldier in him took over and he would sharply point out the insufficiencies, the inadequacies, the weaknesses to the drill master. By heaven, if you had an army, you had an army, not a band of clumsy oafs.

A second Continental Congress had been called for the following May. In the months that preceded it, his dining room became almost a conference hall. Carter and Gates and Lee came; Patrick Henry, Pendleton, Robinson, Mason . . . The talk was quiet and sober. It was on the coming Congress, what decisions would be made, and how much advance preparation could be completed for a speedy enactment of the decisions they felt to be inevitable.

He would have liked to shield Patsy from these conversations but it wasn't possible. She listened and questioned and seemed to weigh and measure. Yet he honestly believed that she was not able to conceive of a real war breaking out but was treating the issue more as a family squabble. She was always outwardly composed and even had begun to laugh at the occasional witticisms that relieved the solemn tone of the gatherings. She remained the unfailingly perfect hostess and his guests always complimented him on his table.

Often the conferences lasted long into the evening and Patsy would excuse herself and slip up to bed. For years they had fallen asleep with her head against his shoulder, both of them enjoying the few minutes of sleepy conversation before one or the other drifted off. Even the nights when she retired first, before little Patsy died, he had automatically slipped an arm around her and drawn her to him. But these nights he retired noiselessly. She always seemed to be asleep, and since waking her might lead to one of the weeping spells that had come so frequently for so many months, he was careful to slip into bed making as little stirring as possible.

Sometimes he would lie awake for hours while with terrible clarity he foresaw the problems that would have to be faced. People did not really understand war unless they had been in it. To too many people, it was uniforms and parades. War was dirt and mud and dysentery and wounds; it was stinking supplies and contaminated water; it was broken bodies and separation from loved ones; it was depletion of fortune; setback in life work; agony and discouragement; jealousy and internal strife. And it was coming.

At this point in his meditations he would start to stretch out his arm, wanting the soft warmth of Patsy against him. Always he withdrew it.

He left for the Congress in May, wearing again the blue-and-red uniform. When it was time to go, Patsy walked to the door with him and came out on the front steps. She had worn so much black clothing for nearly two years that he'd almost forgotten how pleasant it was to see her in colors. She was dressed in a blue morning dress that sparkled in the warmth of her eyes. The hair that had once been a warm lustrous brown was streaked with soft gray, but the gray strands that slipped out from under her cap only gave an appealing young look as they curled around her forehead and ears.

Once she would have clung to him and wept at the prospect of a month's separation. Now, when he took her hand, she stared straight up at him. She seemed to be about to speak, but no words came. She who had wept ten thousand tears for her dead child was dry-eyed now. On the one hand he was grateful for her composure. On the other he wondered if the time had passed when she had tears for him. "I'll write as soon as I arrive in Philadelphia. Good-bye, my dearest," he said.

He kissed her lips and cheek and thought the hand he was still holding trembled, but her "Good-bye, George," was said calmly enough. Aware of Richard

Henry Lee and Jacky near the foot of the stairs, he stepped back and she immediately took her hand from his. The groom came forward quickly with his carriage, and George started down the stairs. This good-bye was unsatisfactory and wrong. He wanted to turn back and hold Patsy tightly against him for just one moment but was afraid he might embarrass her with the others there.

Grimly, he got into the vehicle. He leaned his head out the window and raised his arm in farewell but his good-bye was lost in the hearty ones that the others called to her. They started down the road, but just before they turned out of sight, he looked back. She was still standing there, such a very small figure. The sun was barely coming up now, and the first beams danced against the windows and through the trees that lined the path. The early morning dew was still on the great house and the white paint glistened in the first strong light. He had a presentiment that he would not see Mount Vernon or Patsy again for a long time. He watched with anguished eyes as she waved her hand in a final farewell.

At the inn where they stopped for dinner, Lee told him emotionally what Patsy's admonition to the delegates had been. She confided, "I hope you will all stand firm. I know George will."

When he heard the words, George got up and

walked away from the table. If Patsy could say that to his friends and to her son, why could she not have spoken in a similar vein to him. Why had a chasm come between them at the very hour when their need for each other was greatest?

WHEN HE ARRIVED IN PHILADELPHIA, George found that many of the other members of the Congress had spent the winter mulling over the same sobering thoughts that he himself had considered. It was all very well to talk of rights, but the Colonies were poor. They were divided into sections, and there were many who considered George III the rightful ruler. There were many who saw as folly the pitting of a mouse against a tiger with almost certain ruin as the result.

And yet, after all the negative elements had been considered, most of the delegates shared the hard, inflexible inner conviction that would not permit despotism. They probably would lose all they had in the struggle, but at least it would be lost with honor.

Pro and con, wearying detail, patriotism and wrangling . . . George listened and observed; he approved the resolution to raise and send companies to Boston for the relief of that beleaguered city. Even as he voiced his approval, he was painfully aware that he was the only del-

egate in uniform and his military background was the subject of intense discussion.

On June 14 the debate over the choice of a commander for the American troops began. When George
heard John Adams begin his speech, he nodded in agree-
ment. Adams was saying that if relief were not sent to
the Colonial forces currently besieging the British outside Boston, and if that army were permitted to dissolve,
a new one might never be raised. Adams slammed his
hand against a desk to emphasize his point. "The time is
now to present a united front to the King," he thundered.

Then, in a calmer voice, he began his proposal for the
man he believed best suited to be commander in chief of
the colonists. With growing dismay George listened as he
realized the short and outspoken Adams was talking
about him. Heads turned in his direction and finally he
stood up and quietly left the room. In God's name, if they
were going to discuss his assets and liabilities as a military
leader, his presence would be a bone in the throat.

He returned to his lodging house and stayed there all
that day and most of the next. He knew that in all likeli-
hood his name would be acceptable to the delegates and
he would be chosen to command the troops. His honesty
made him face that fact; his humility questioned his ability to complete the task. In the day and a half that he
stayed in his rooms he went over his affairs mentally, jot-

ting down notes on any tasks that needed completing. If he were chosen to go to the Boston area, he would make out a new will. A man could die as easily in a skirmish as in a battle and his old will was no longer suitable.

He resigned himself to the fact that if he should be appointed, he would have to go directly to Boston. No matter how much he desired it, a visit to Mount Vernon would be impossible. Maybe the separation would only be for a few months. Possibly, if the King saw the determination of the Colonies to stand together, a speedy and just reconciliation would take place. Then he could be home by Christmas. And possibly the siege of Boston was only the harbinger of months and even years of battles ahead.

He would have to write to Patsy if he were not coming home. How could he tell her? Why had they not somehow resolved the sadness between them before he left? Pacing the room, George thought of the fourteen happy years that had ended when little Patsy died. In these past months he'd been so concerned about the affairs of the Colonies, was it possible that he failed his wife? Would Patsy have turned to him as she came out of that first terrible grief if he had not been so very involved with the meetings and the drills and the problems of government? Perhaps, even if he had been little Patsy's natural father, Patsy would have had the same exclusive attitude about her grief. Mothers always did consider their feelings were deepest where children were concerned. Fathers were rather always pushed aside.

But then there was the whole business of Jacky and college and marriage. His opinion and advice were simply ignored there. It would be so much easier if he didn't care, so much easier if he felt the part of the stepfather and second husband. But long ago he had managed to stamp out his romantic love for Sally because it was the very need of his nature to be first in the life of his beloved. The need to be first had helped him to redeem the disaster of Monongahela. It had sustained him in his unending effort to transform Mount Vernon from a small house on limited acreage to a mansion on a plantation.

Then why could he not be first with his wife, the very soul and center of his being?

A knock came at the door and George slowly walked to open it. Several of the delegates were waiting to address him. Their greeting was the one he had expected and dreaded to hear. With an air of bringing great tidings they said, "Good evening, General."

After they had left, George went for a long walk. He would be leaving immediately for Cambridge. Would Patsy miss him? Of course she would. He'd write to Jacky and Nellie and tell them to go to Mount Vernon to stay with her. Thank heaven for Lund, who was a good overseer. Between him and Patsy they could run Mount Vernon.

It was a warm and muggy evening. He walked up the streets and down quiet lanes. He passed a dry-goods shop with brightly colored material displayed in the window. One pattern with blue flowers scattered on a white background caught his eye. George hesitated a moment, then peered inside the window. The shopkeeper was still there. He went to the door, opened it, and stepped inside. A few minutes later he emerged with enough of the goods for a dress for Patsy. The proprietor had assured him that this was, by far, the prettiest pattern he'd ever laid his eyes on in the Colonies, and George agreed. Patsy would wear the gown this summer at Mount Vernon.

But he would not be there to see her.

H E LEFT IN THE MORNING OF JUNE 23 on his trip toward Boston. He had bought a new phaeton and had sent the carriage back to Mount Vernon, but as usual he began the trip on horseback. It was easier to think, to plan, when he was outside, when he held reins in his hands, when he had the immediate choice of hastening or slowing. His company included his new aides Thomas Mifflin and Joseph Reed, and two of his generals, Charles Lee and Philip Schuyler.

The journey to Cambridge took one week. In Newark and New York, in New Rochelle and New Haven—all along the way he was cheered to see the enthusiastic response the local inhabitants gave him. The news that companies of militia were springing up all through the Colonies was reassuring.

But when they finally arrived at Cambridge, it was raining and no one knew quite when to expect them. It seemed to him symbolic of the end of fanfare and the beginning of war to arrive at his final destination, mud-spattered, unheralded, and unwelcomed.

The irritations began immediately. The very first order of business came when he found that he and his officers were to stay in the house of Samuel Langdon, the president of Harvard College, while the owner was confined to one room. Washington listened to the arrangements and quietly decided to find another house immediately.

Long ago he had chafed because a royal commission could outweigh his own similar rank as a Continental. He wasn't surprised to learn at once that there was widespread grumbling about appointments in the American Army now. The New England generals had cause for grievance. Some of the best men had been made the juniors of the officers whom they had commanded in the Massachusetts forces—and the reversal was the result of stupidity on the part of the Congress.

The first days at Cambridge spread daylight on the enormous task that lay before him. The English were securely in charge of Boston, but the geography of the area gave the Continentals protection against a surprise attack. He found more gunpowder than he'd been led to expect, and fewer guns. The fortifications were pitifully inadequate. If the British had any idea how poor they really were, they'd settle the whole affair immediately with an all-out attack.

He found more men in the army than he'd counted

on. He knew from the Bunker Hill battle that they were brave. He also found them ill-kempt, undisciplined, and untrained.

George realized there would be no immediate confrontation. His task would be to maintain the siege on Boston but without direct attack. In the meantime he would try to make an army out of the Continentals.

He moved to a new headquarters, the confiscated house of a loyalist. There, surrounded by his official family, he undertook the job of creating an army. Daily he expected a surprise attack from the British. The fact that the "lobsters," as his men called the redcoats, made absolutely no overt attack led to a new and even grimmer worry. Were the British simply planning to wait them out, letting them feed and drill nearly twenty thousand men until winter drove them into scattering? Would this be a war won in the accounting house and the granary?

He fed and drilled nineteen thousand men each week and the only action most of them saw was an occasional skirmish.

Fall came to New England. During the rare breaks George permitted himself in his long days he would lay down his pen and walk to the window to observe the glorious yellows, oranges, greens, and browns of the New England landscape. He often longed to go out and take a walk in the chill bracing air, just as at Mount Vernon he often walked from the house down the steep bank through the woods to the low sandy shore of the Potomac.

The vivid beauty of New England filled him with pride. To him no place on earth would ever have the beauty of his own acres, but in the first weeks he lived in Cambridge he came to appreciate the pretty town, the handsome farms, and the relentless unabating struggle the farmers had to wrest crops from the hard soil.

New Englanders had a strength, a hard core of resistance that probably was the result of this bracing climate.

North to south, New England farms to southern plantations, it was a land worth fighting for, a land that even without oppression would have eventually outgrown the role of son in the father's house.

During the moments when he stood, his palms pressed against the windowsills, staring out into the fall afternoons, George could feel the burdens and worry easing. It was as though he could look into the future: a future when the thirteen Colonies would push their boundaries westward, when yet unborn surveyors would stake off new land from virgin forests. The British Empire was ruled by a tiny island. How much more promise of mightiness these Colonies had, when eventually they could hope to expand on their own continent.

Then he would go back to his desk, heartened and even more conscious of his role. He was not simply commander in chief of the revolutionary Colonies. He was one of the planters Providence had chosen to see that the mustard seed of a great nation was sown safely.

It was this thought that helped him maintain an air of quiet confidence around his staff and before the troops. No one was permitted to see the total picture as he saw it: the hopelessly dark overall weakness of the Colonial forces.

He heard from Lund and Patsy frequently. They both wrote as though they understood what he wanted to hear. Patsy told him about the doings at home. She gave a feminine viewpoint on the progress of the additions to the house. She kept him informed about which mares had foaled and wrote gossipy news about the slaves.

She wrote with enthusiasm about their new bedroom. She had had their furniture moved into it and was already occupying it. "It is very handsome," she wrote, "and I am sure you will be very pleased. The view is fine no matter what the weather. The furniture fits very well and the greater dimension of this room does it far more justice. The carpet has been laid with care. The dressing rooms are well-situated. You will enjoy the convenience of yours, I know. In truth, the whole feeling of these new quarters is so right for you that at night, when I lay in bed, I find myself waiting for your footstep."

In his first letter telling her he would not be returning he had begged her not to voice unhappiness because it would be too distressing to him. He had never received a single complaining letter. She did not really say that she missed him. But "at night she lay waiting for his footstep." He wondered about those many nights that he had gone to their room and assumed she was asleep. Perhaps after all she had been awake. Was it possible that he might somehow have appeared to be showing pique at her continued mourning?

He had felt that she did not consider him enough. Yet all her letters read, "You will be pleased to know"; "I think you will like"; "I smiled when I thought of your probable reaction to . . ."

It was as though she was seeing life through his eyes. Wasn't that proof of love? He wanted to see Patsy. His need for her permeated his very being.

Lund kept him closely informed of overall developments at home. Lord Dunmore, the British governor of Virginia, had retreated with his family onto a British man-of-war and was threatening to shell the houses along the Potomac.

Lund thought he should put off further work on the additions. If the house were burned, it would mean lost labor and a frightful waste of money. His papers were being packed away and taken to a safe place. The overseer added that Mrs. Washington had undertaken that task herself.

And then the message came that sent icy dread

through George. Lund was worried about Patsy. He noti-
fied George that many Virginians believed Dunmore was
planning to raze Mount Vernon and capture the wife of
the commander in chief as a prisoner of war.

George's first reaction to the letter was disbelief. Lord
Dunmore was an aristocrat. Every instinct assured George
that he was too much the gentleman to wage war against
a helpless woman. No. He would not deliberately attempt
to harm Patsy. But Mount Vernon was something else.
His own inordinate pride in the plantation was a source of
respect and amusement to his friends. Certainly it was
well-known to Dunmore.

Why wouldn't he in his rage shatter what it had taken
General Washington years to build? After all he,
Washington, was trying to tear down the system to which
Dunmore was dedicated. And if Dunmore shelled Mount
Vernon, Patsy might be in it.

Oh, granted, Lund assured him that they had plans
to spirit her away, that within ten minutes of sighting a
ship she could be on her way to a prepared hiding place
with friends. George knew that sometimes these ten-
minute warnings simply did not exist. A vessel could slip
up in a heavy fog and begin shelling before an alarm
could be sounded.

The thought made the lines across his forehead
deepen and his air of reserve become more pronounced.

Soon he was receiving tactful hints from his aide, Reed, that the commander in chief was felt to be haughty and aloof. Perhaps he could unbend a little.

George found that if he relaxed at all, it was at the dinners or gatherings when some of the wives of his staff officers would lend a touch of gaiety and pleasure to the atmosphere. He especially enjoyed pretty Kitty Greene, the wife of one of his most trusted officers, Nathanael Greene. Kitty was the niece of a prominent Rhode Island legislator. She was desperately in love with grave Nat Greene but still just a bit of a natural flirt. She would start an evening by being very deferential to George, and then her natural humor would bubble up and he'd find himself laughing at her quips.

The minute the music started at the gatherings, her foot would begin tapping. One evening she curtsied to him and said, "Your Excellency, rumor has it that you are the finest dancer in all Virginia. May I help you prove worthy of that reputation?"

George laughed and jumped to his feet. Nat Greene shook his head at his wife, even while he laughed, too. It had been months since George danced but it was still as natural to him as walking or riding. Even steps that he didn't know, he could instinctively pick up by simply glancing at the feet of the others on the floor.

Kitty was an exquisite partner, light and graceful.

Suddenly he realized whom she reminded him of. Dear God, she was so like Sally twenty years ago. And Nat Greene, unable to enjoy the dancing because of his stiff knee, might have been George William sitting on the side with his rheumatism.

The comparison made George enjoy the dance all the more keenly. The musicians, seeing his pleasure, kept playing long after they normally would have stopped. One by one the other couples dropped out until only he and Kitty danced. Finally, when she was flushed and out of breath, he deposited her at her husband's side.

"I confess to being a shade out of practice tonight," he said gravely. "But one evening we must see how long we can go. It is quite good to take one's measure, even on the dance floor."

Kitty recovered her breath enough to reply with equal gravity, "Your Excellency, may I assure you that your reputation as the best dancer in Virginia is quite deserved. And in all New England I have never had such a partner."

It was a rewarding evening. The feeling of good humor and pleasure stayed with George until he retired. Billy had the bed warmed and the covers turned down. Billy was waiting to pull off his boots and take his jacket. But Billy was not the one he wanted there. He wanted Patsy with him. He wanted to be able to ask her whom she thought Kitty Greene resembled, and of course she would know. He wanted to bait her by gravely suggesting that young Hamilton was a distinct asset to the cause. He knew that the man's combination of cocksureness and haughty manners would irritate Patsy no end. George thought of how much he had always relished Patsy's penetrating observations about people. They helped to clear and focus his own impressions.

After Billy left the room George sighed and stood up. He was dead tired but restless and suddenly out of sorts. Already it was November and Christmas was coming soon. What kind of Christmas would it be like here, so far from home?

Unless . . . unless, since he could not go to her at Mount Vernon, Patsy could come here to join him. Immediately George rejected the thought as impossible. It was too cold and too late in the year. The roads would be bad and Patsy had never been north of Virginia in her life.

But hours later as he still lay awake, George came to a decision. In the morning he would write Patsy and ask her to come to him.

December, 1775
Cambridge

HE NEXT MORNING WHEN HE WROTE, George was careful to couch his invitation to Patsy in the most negative of tones. He took an almost perverse pride in making it easy for her not to come. He pointed out that the roads were bad and it was late in the season. She was probably enjoying a visit to her sister Nancy Bassett and the company of her relatives. New England would be a cold, snowy place to spend Christmas.

At the same time he wrote a note to Lund saying that he'd invited Patsy, but didn't expect her.

It would be weeks at least before he could hope for word. George spent nearly every waking hour of those weeks totally absorbed in the grim struggle to hold together his army. Many enlistments ended in December. Here, after months of training and feeding troops, he must now release them without having obtained one single piece of good from them.

The plight of General Arnold in Canada and the disaster of that campaign added to his woes. Wood was so scarce that it was impossible to keep enough of a supply on hand to build barracks and have fuel as well.

At night just before he fell asleep he would finally for a few minutes turn his thoughts away from the war and permit himself to wonder what Patsy's answer would be. Over and over he relived the moment when he had said good-bye to her. He should have embraced her and not worried about the presence of the others.

Quite against his wishes he felt his temper grow increasingly shorter. He must not take either public or private problems out on his staff. He willed himself to external serenity, even while the slightest exhibition of stupidity or carelessness triggered hot emotion.

Then simultaneously he heard from Patsy and Lund. She was coming, coming as fast as a carriage could be raced along the snowy path from Virginia to Cambridge. In her letter, hastily scrawled, even more badly spelled than usual, she said simply, "If you had not sent for me, I should still have come to you."

From Lund there was much the same news. Mrs. Washington had long been saying that she would go to the general if he could not come home. Mrs. Washington had all the slaves near collapse with preparing food to take to Cambridge. Mrs. Washington would be on her way in a few days. Mrs. Washington would be accompanied by Mr. and Mrs. Custis.

Exhilaration was followed by acute awareness of the Cambridge house as it would be seen through Patsy's eyes. George thought of his bedroom. He had noticed dust in the corners between the wall and ceiling. That had better be attended to before Patsy got here. During the day when he was busy, she'd need a room to receive guests—oh, the small parlor across the hall. That would do. For Christmas—with any luck she would arrive by then—he'd get the men to cut boughs from the evergreens and mistletoe. Patsy must get the flavor of a real New England Christmas.

Finally he turned to the papers on his desk. Wood was still scarce. The Connecticut regiments could not be prevailed upon to reenlist. A traitor had slipped through to Boston and told the British that this was exactly the right time to attack. There was serious reason to believe that Dr. Church had been sending messages to the enemy.

But George treated each crisis that day with calm assurance. When moments of discouragement came, he had only to think of the carriage that even now was probably close to Philadelphia.

He wrote to Reed to escort Patsy into Philadelphia and attend her during her few days' stopover there. For the last part of the trip he sent Colonel Baylor to meet and guide the carriage through New England.

He told the ladies—Kitty Greene and Mercy

Warren and Mrs. Mifflin—that she was coming, and they assured him that they would see she did not become lonesome when he was busy.

On the evening of December 11 he was in his study, poring over the interminable reports to the Congress. For the past few days he'd had one ear cocked for the sound of carriage wheels, but now he became so absorbed in trying to phrase his words properly that he tuned out extraneous sounds. He needed to make the Congress understand the desperation of their plight, but he must not seem desperate. Discouragement was not the emotion he must give them, rather an awareness of need, with confidence in ultimate victory.

He heard the front door open and the sound of hurrying feet. He rose quickly as a sentry tapped on the door and rushed in. "She is here, Your Excellency, your lady is here."

George brushed past the man. He covered the long hall in a few strides. The front door was being held open by another sentry. He raced down the steps. The carriage was at the foot of the double stairs. Jacky was standing beside it, handing Nellie out. He gave his stepson a gentle touch and the young man stepped quickly aside.

George lifted his arms up and Patsy stepped from the carriage into them.

He held her against him, his arms tight around her

waist and back, her gloved hands folded around his neck. He kissed the smooth cheek and her eyes and lips. She was here. She was here. She had come through ice and snow and danger and risked capture to come to him, but she had come. Whatever his place in her affections, he would accept it. She was always and ever first in his. And she was here. She murmured his name and he tried to say "welcome, my dearest," but his voice was so low he wondered if she heard. Keeping an arm around her, he brought her into the house. Finally he left her side long enough to greet Jacky and Nellie. Jacky had become a man, nearly two years of marriage had given him a purposeful expression, a maturity that sat well on his handsome frame. Nellie was as lovely as ever and showed a self-assurance that had been lacking in the ecstatic new bride.

George pumped Jacky's hand, hugged and kissed Nellie quickly, and turned back to Patsy. She had taken off her cloak and bonnet and was wearing a handsome dark green traveling dress. In the seven months since he'd seen her, her hair had become completely silver. Was it the hair or her manner? There was an indefinable change in Patsy. There was a regal dignity about her as she handed an aide her cloak. There was a serenity that he'd never noticed before. Once she would have been embarrassed at any affectionate display before the children. Now she came over to him and slipped her hand in his, and Jacky and Nellie might not have been in the room.

Billy brought wine in and greeted the newcomers with a grin that stretched from ear to ear. "Have you been taking good care of the general?" Patsy asked him, smiling.

She accepted the wine and replied to his assurances, "I think the general looks quite well, although he could do with a bit more rest. I see some unfamiliar lines." She ran her finger over his forehead gently. "I don't remember these."

"There are others that show up even more at my desk," George said, "and others that reveal themselves when I review the troops, still others when I look from the hill into Boston Harbor . . . but never mind that now. Tell me about your trip."

Jacky laughed. "Our trip was three weeks of Mamma urging the coachman to hurry. Sir, you can't imagine how happy I am to deliver her to you."

George raised one eyebrow as Patsy said, "Be quiet, Jacky."

Jacky was not to be silenced. "Really, Poppa, ever since the letter came announcing that you would not be returning, Mamma has been driving herself, and everyone else, until I became convinced collapse was the only end. In fact, at Mount Vernon she is every day riding with Lund to see that your instructions are carried out. Every bush you wanted planted, she is there to see it's put in just the spot you indicated. She's a veritable foreman at the additions and all one hears is 'the general will not be pleased; do that over; the general definitely said to trim the corner in such and such a manner.' When your new private quarters were being fixed, she supervised every tack in the carpet, saying that you would notice shoddiness. When everyone pleaded with her to leave Mount Vernon, for fear of Dunmore, she refused. And I doubt, sir, that if that scoundrel had come to the door, she would have fled. She would have said, 'George has put his whole life into Mount Vernon, and I shall save it for him.'"

"What weapons would she have chosen?" George asked mildly. He looked down at Patsy, at the faint blush that painted her cheeks, and was not aware of the tears in his own eyes.

The half-bantering tone left Jacky's voice. "I think love would have been her sword and shield, Poppa," he said quietly. "Now . . ." He touched Nellie's elbow. "We will get ourselves settled and rejoin you a little later for dinner."

Then he stepped to George and grasped his hand. "We have all missed you terribly, sir. If I may, I should like to be of some assistance to you here. It seems entirely wrong for my father to bear the entire responsibility for our forces while I sit idle in Virginia. Perhaps you have some post where I may be of service."

George looked at the handsome young man who had long ago asked to wear his sword. He had been wrong about the early marriage. It had begun the maturing process that he had longed to see in the youth. Jacky had said "my father." Jacky had come not simply as an escort, but to help. "I shall be proud to have you with me," he said. Tomorrow, he thought, tomorrow when I ride to the lines, Jacky will ride with me. Tomorrow the army will see my son.

Then the door was closed behind Nellie and Jacky, and he and Patsy were alone. He thought of what Jacky had said, "love would have been her sword and shield." A tidal wave of emotion swept over him. He blew his nose vigorously, then said, "This parlor . . . I thought you might use it during the day. You could receive the ladies here. I hope it pleases you."

They were facing each other—she in the center of the room. He had walked with the young couple to the door and was standing in front of it. The color had drained from her face and she was dead white now. She clasped her hands tightly together. "The room pleases me very much," she said. "I have missed you, George." They were six feet apart. But it might have been a chasm. The only time he had been this immobilized was that agonizing moment when he held little Patsy in his arms and tried to husband the flicker of life. This moment had that same sense of imminence. Whatever they said now would guide the course of their future. She must understand now how he felt about her. But words would not come.

It was she who spoke first. "Since that morning that you left . . . and I never even said good-bye, did I . . . not really . . . you see, I had been so unhappy that you were going. I needed you. But never considered your needs. Just as you left, I realized . . . I knew that if war came you might not come back. And I knew that I couldn't bear that. Not ever. But I was so selfish last year. I have always been so selfish."

He could not move. He could not answer her. Reassuring words crowded his throat. "You were not selfish. You were grief-stricken." But he couldn't say them.

She took one step toward him. "All these months I have been thinking. How happy little Patsy was. How happy you made her. When she was ill and frightened, it was always you she turned to. From that very first minute when she reached out to you, when she was just a baby, you protected her. You cared for her. You gave her all the happiness, all the love. You made her life perfect. And when she died I never once thought of you, only of myself . . ."

Another step. Now her voice was breathless. Words were tumbling out. "And all these years . . . Jacky . . . you arranging for the schools, getting him out of scrapes, mak-

ing a man out of him when I would have ruined him. You
know who told me that? He did. He did. And his wedding—wanting him to get married so he'd be around me
more, wanting grandchildren, instead of worrying about
you when you were so worried. I never gave you a child of
your own and you never reproached me, not once. You were
sorry for my disappointment, and all alone you have carried
so much weight on your shoulders these months . . ."

She was in front of him now, her hands on his chest.
She twisted the button on his jacket. "I wanted to come
long ago, but I was afraid you might not want me. When
you wrote that Mrs. Greene and Mrs. Mifflin and the
others were here, and never once asked me to come, I
thought that maybe . . . I had become a burden. I would
have come soon anyhow. I would have had to. Only the
chance to be watching over Mount Vernon for you has
given any meaning to my life these months . . ."

The button came off. Absently she tucked it in his
pocket then went on. "I have been very difficult and very
sharp. Everyone thinks so. I know it. It is just that when
you aren't there, it's all wrong. I have missed you so much.
It isn't any pleasure to ride or walk or dine or visit, if
you're not there. And so I get cross and notice mistakes
and get very irritated."

She was working on the next button, twisting and
tugging at it. "And all I have been able to think, all I have

lived with, is the thought that if we are defeated, they would hang you. They would, wouldn't they? And I simply could not bear . . ." The button popped off. She stared at it, suddenly aware of what she was doing. She looked up at him, startled and blushing. "Oh, George . . ."

And now the frozen emotion was gone. Warmth coursed through his body. Now he could move. Now he could speak. They laughed together as he held her against him. "My dearest, dearest Patsy." Their tears wet each other's cheeks as he kissed her. "I am so proud of you," she whispered. In unison they said, "I love you."

And then because the others would be joining them soon for supper—Jacky and Nellie and the staff officers—she dried her eyes, smoothed her hair, and reached into her pocket for the needle and thread she always carried and began to sew the buttons back on. He sat by her as she did, content and rejoicing.

How many nights they had sat like this at home . . . and they would again. He was sure of it. No matter how long it took, and it would take a long time, no matter what the hardships, and there would be many, no matter how great the pain, and pain and grief were part of war, they would succeed.

Tonight he would tell her about it all. Tonight when they would fall asleep with her head on his shoulder. He would warn her. But she already knew. She could stay until spring. And when the campaign started, he would send her home. But she would be with him whenever it was possible. Newfound energy made him forget the fatigue and the worry and the strain. All his life he had waited for these last few minutes . . . all his life.

She finished her sewing and motioned him to stand up. She held his jacket while he slipped his arms into the sleeves. She said, "The general looks very handsome," and investigated her handwork. She said, "They're sewed quite secure, I think. In fact, they're probably more secure than before."

"I have no doubt of it," he said gravely. "And now . . ."

"His Excellency is hungry," she guessed.

"Starving!" He had never been so hungry in his life, and drifting through the house was the tantalizing aroma of the ham and pies that Patsy had brought from Mount Vernon.

THE BALTIMORE ESCORT RODE WITH THEM to the Fountain Inn where they were to stay. Outside the establishment and on the streets leading to it an enormous crowd waited to greet them. The snowstorm was thick and the wind drove swirling flakes past mufflers and cloaks against their necks and throats. George was frantic to get Patsy out of the cold, but she would not be hurried as she smiled and bowed to the throngs.

At his whispered insistence that she go indoors, she said calmly, "These people have stood for hours to see us. Surely we can stand outside for just a few minutes."

Mayor Calhoun had a speech prepared but, considerately, shortened it and contented himself with giving them the compliments of the Council of Baltimore.

They were on their way early the next morning and the bad weather pursued them to their next stop at Bladensburg. But when they arrived on the fourteenth in the new federal city of Washington, the snow had begun to melt and the roads were a veritable sea of mud. The horses strained to pull the carriage as the wheels sank into the endless ruts. George looked out the carriage window eagerly. He wasn't sorry that his administration had ended before the government moved to this new site. It was for the Adams family to occupy the residence that would be the new Executive Mansion. He was glad that the task of settling it hadn't fallen on Patsy's shoulders.

That afternoon they had dinner with Patty and Thomas Peter, then all went to the home of Eliza and Thomas Law for supper. En route they passed the partially built Executive Mansion and in that area they were rendered a sixteen-gun salute. Patsy studied the dimensions of the house eagerly. "It will be so beautiful," she said, "and so worthy a backdrop for the office, but I am pleased to be spared the task of making it a home."

Just what he had thought an hour ago, George reflected. It showed that after forty years of marriage even their thinking had become identical.

Eliza Law and Patty Peter were the older daughters of Nellie and Jacky Custis. At dinner George noticed how delighted his Patsy was to be at table with all three of her granddaughters. The girls were such fine young women and like their brother, young Washington, they each bore a great resemblance to their father.

Of course, of the three girls, George admitted to

himself that Nelly was his favorite. But that was understandable, he felt. They'd raised her from babyhood. Patsy was listening intently to the girls as they discussed their decorating efforts in their new homes. Both of the two older sisters were recent brides. Someone joked that Nelly would be the next to choose a husband and then everyone laughed and George knew it was because he looked so dismayed.

"Grandpapa doesn't want to lose Nelly," Eliza said.

"Grandpapa is only aware of the trail of belongings Nelly has lost on this trip and thinks she had better wait a bit before she loses her heart, too," he retorted.

Nelly got up and slipped an arm around his neck. She gave him a quick kiss on the top of his head. "You are just cross because I forgot the parrots," she said.

Her grandmother's hearty laugh led the rest.

Later, after they had retired to the comfortable and well-appointed bed chamber, George found that he could not sleep. The nearness to Mount Vernon filled him with such exhilaration that all hope for immediate rest seemed wasted. Quietly, so as not to disturb Patsy, he got out of bed and went to sit in the armchair by the window. At night the stark newness of the city wasn't visible. At night the silhouettes of half-completed buildings were symbols of promise.

What would this city—this city they had named after him—be like in a decade, a generation, a hundred years? Usually it was better not to know the future, but for this country he would like a chance to see what the next century would bring. Surely there would be struggles and setbacks and failures, but in the end this nation would become mighty. It had the freshness and the vigor of youth. It had the stamina of a dedicated and great-hearted people.

How he had witnessed the heart and courage of that people—at Cambridge and New York, at Trenton and Saratoga, at Valley Forge and Yorktown. He'd watched his men starving and ragged, uncomplaining as they preserved the dream and pursued the struggle. Until, at last, at the great victory at Yorktown, Cornwallis had surrendered his sword.

George sighed restlessly and got up to look out the window. But he wasn't seeing the moon-bathed federal city. Instead he was in the plain at Yorktown again, with his army assembled, and accepting the British surrender from the officer representing Cornwallis. They had struggled more than seven years from the first days at Cambridge to that October morning in 1781 when the British band played "The World Turned Upside Down," as their defeated officers marched from the field. The significance of that air seemed to have been lost on the redcoats. It was the music to which the Continentals sang their jaunty tune "Yankee Doodle Dandy"!

In the thousands of eyes that were on him in those fate-filled moments he was sadly reminded of Jacky's absence.

Involuntarily George tightened his hands into fists. Even after sixteen years it was hard to think of his stepson without experiencing a terrible pang of loss. He thought of the times Jacky had been at his side at Yorktown, serving as his trusted aide. The laziness and indolence of adolescence had been an incongruous contrast to the young man who had matured into a devoted husband, father, and son. The only thing that hadn't changed in those days was the quick Custis wit. George remembered the hundreds of times that Jacky had managed to make him smile even in the very blackest of moments. But then the ill health that seemed to be a heritage of the Custis children came to the surface as the long hours and privations weakened Jacky's reserve of strength. Camp fever swept over Jacky in full force and he was taken to the home of Patsy's sister in Eltham, some thirty miles away. Patsy and Nellie came to take care of him, but then George received a frantic message: Jacky was dying.

He arrived in time to be at the bedside of the boy who had been his son. He held Jacky's hand as the long, shuddering sighs became fainter and finally stopped. Afraid of what he would see, he turned to Patsy. But she was not looking down at her son's body. Instead her arms were tight around Nellie, and she was whispering consolation to the distraught young widow. George embraced them both and then had to hurry back to Yorktown. In the midst of his sorrow one comforting thought was like a candle in the gloom. This time Patsy would be all right. This time she would spend her grief by helping to care for Nellie and Jacky's fatherless children.

The great victory had been achieved but the state of war wasn't over. Nearly two years of skirmishes and waiting were to follow before the peace treaty was signed and he was able to resign his commission and go home.

Patsy let no hint of the sorrow of losing her only son mar his homecoming. A party air pervaded the house and from far and wide neighbors and relatives were invited to welcome him home. He realized that somehow she had made her peace with the fate that had made her long-ago nightmare of four tombstones for her four children come true.

But Mount Vernon was not to be without children. When Nellie returned to her home, she took her two older girls but left the babies, little Nelly and little

Washington, behind. She asked them to care for the younger children, saying that Mount Vernon should have youngsters to enjoy it, and she knew it would please Jacky if his mother and the general were to help raise his family.

Generous, understanding Nellie—how kind she had been to surrender her own natural desire to raise her children. She had remarried a few years after that to George's great friend, Dr. David Stewart. The Stewarts had a large family now, but Nellie always remained very close to her Custis children.

With understanding and love Patsy had blessed her former daughter-in-law's second marriage, saying, "She made Jacky very happy and deserves happiness again herself. And, besides, whatever would my life have been if, as a young widow, I had not remarried?"

The very bewilderment in the question made George smile. "And what would I have done if you had not remarried?" he had asked mildly.

"George!" A firm and disapproving voice made him turn around with guilty haste. Patsy was sitting up in bed, frowning. "Come to bed, immediately. You'll have a chill."

Meekly the general obeyed, realizing that he was indeed chilled and cramped. He pulled the covers up, aware that this bed was not quite long enough for him to stretch out comfortably, and lamely began an explanation. "I found I couldn't sleep and began to think."

"You most certainly didn't think about your throat," Patsy retorted, but now the firmness in her voice was giving way to worry. "See how cold your hands are." She began to massage them.

"I hadn't noticed. I was thinking about the war years and how after it was all over I thought I was going home for good."

"And you looked just as tired then as you do now. But a few weeks at home will be all you will need. And, thank heaven, this time there's no chance they'll be trying to call you back. I think you can count on being Farmer Washington, old man."

He leaned back against the pillow and closed his eyes. "I can't imagine a title I'd treasure more. How I have hated to trade it for others."

"I remember when Farmer Washington learned he was to be President Washington," Patsy said. "I think that was one time when I accepted the inevitable before you did. As soon as the Constitution was written, I had not the slightest doubt who would be chosen as the first President."

"Adams received many electoral votes," George reminded her.

"Adams never received serious consideration," Patsy said firmly. "And now, old man, will you please go to sleep? There is still so much traveling to do before we get home."

"No, Patsy," he said exultantly, "that's just the point. There's so little traveling to do. We're almost finished with the journey."

He felt the heaviness of sleep weigh on his eyelids. It would have been interesting to continue to meditate, to go over the last eight years, but he'd have time for that. Already it was suggested that he spend his retirement writing an autobiography. An autobiography, indeed! His limited education would lend itself to no such venture. Let others tell the story for him. Historians would record the tale of his two administrations. Some, like journalist Bache, would find his stewardship a disaster. Others might understand that he had tried according to the light that had been given him and might, indeed, find merit in his efforts and achievements.

Time again, time would tell; time would record and weigh and balance. He had tried his best and he would content himself with that knowledge. Oh, he knew about his failures, there had been enough of those. As he drifted off to sleep, he decided that even his mother would probably admit that he hadn't too greatly diminished her family's motto. His last waking thought was the memory of his mother's voice repeating that motto to her children, "Aspire . . . to . . . the . . . heavens."

The next morning they started early. Georgetown was waiting to receive them with escorts and parades and addresses. Then came Alexandria and now the excitement made them all speechless. It was windy and cold but the sun was high in the sky. Spring was ready to burst forth behind the last frigid blasts of winter.

Finally they were just a few miles from Mount Vernon. The ferry landing was filled with people waiting for them, but this gathering was different from the others. These were neighbors and townspeople who had come not to receive a President but to welcome one of their own who was coming home for good. They shouted huzzahs and greetings and mounted their horses to escort the carriages on the last lap of the journey.

The road that led to Mount Vernon also led to Belvoir. Patsy's eyes had a reflective expression. George knew that she was sharing his thoughts. South, then east on this road. How often they had taken it to visit the Fairfaxes. But Belvoir had been destroyed during the war. George William was dead and Sally would probably never return. George felt Patsy's hand slip into his. How perfect this homecoming would have been if those two old friends had been here to greet them as they had so long ago.

They were on Mount Vernon land, their land. The carriage picked up momentum; the horses literally flew until they were finally within sight of the house. There it was! It gleamed magnificent and proud in the late afternoon sun. Lights shone from every window like welcoming beacons. The carriage rode around the new bowling green as slaves hurried to gather in the courtyard. They spilled out from the stable and the spinning house, from the kitchen and the carpenter's shop. On the steps the house servants in the scarlet-and-stone Washington livery waved their hands in greeting. Voices called their names and cried their welcome.

The townspeople who had escorted them home scrambled from their mounts and joined in the cheers. Slowly, deliberately, George helped Patsy out of the carriage. He knew that the brightness of her eyes was reflected in his own. Swallowing hard, he turned to greet his friends and cordially invite them in. But they would not come. They shook hands and smiled and promised to return soon. They rode off and he and Patsy greeted the slaves, who fairly beamed with joy.

Old Billy was there to meet them and it was he who had the honor of opening the door to admit them. He began to close it but George reached out and took the knob in his own strong grasp. He gave a final glance at the land—the land that in the morning he would be inspecting and caring for again, then quietly and firmly he closed the door. The sharp winter air left a latent chill in the foyer, but he and Patsy went quickly into the parlor where a roaring fire was waiting to welcome home the master of Mount Vernon. 🅀

Visit

MARY HIGGINS CLARK

At the Simon & Schuster Web site:

www.SimonSays.com/mhclark

Read excerpts from her books, find a listing of future titles, and learn more about the author!

SIMON & SCHUSTER
A VIACOM COMPANY
www.SimonSays.com

Pocket
Books

Visit the
Simon & Schuster Web site:
www.SimonSays.com

and sign up for our
mystery e-mail updates!

Keep up on the latest
new releases, author appearances,
news, chats, special offers, and more!
We'll deliver the information
right to your inbox — if it's new,
you'll know about it.